Henry Clarke Wright

The Empire of the Mother

Over the character and destiny of the race

Henry Clarke Wright

The Empire of the Mother
Over the character and destiny of the race

ISBN/EAN: 9783337272821

Printed in Europe, USA, Canada, Australia, Japan

Cover: Foto ©Andreas Hilbeck / pixelio.de

More available books at **www.hansebooks.com**

THE

EMPIRE OF THE MOTHER

OVER

THE CHARACTER AND DESTINY
OF THE RACE.

BY HENRY C. WRIGHT,

Author of "Marriage and Parentage," "The Unwelcome Child," "A Kiss for a Blow,"
"The Self-Abnegationist, or Earth's True King and Queen."

The Health of Woman — the Hope of the World.

SECOND EDITION.

BOSTON:
PUBLISHED BY BELA MARSH, 14 BROMFIELD STREET.
1866.

PREFACE.

In considering Man and his Destiny, I view him in three states; (1) in that which intervenes between conception and birth, which I call his *pre-natal* state; (2) in that which intervenes between his birth and the death of his body, which I call his *post-natal* state; (3) and in that which begins at the death of the body, and never ends, which I call his *disembodied* state; or, *his life within the veil.*

The following pages relate to the first, or pre-natal state. Efforts, whose object is to secure to man a healthy and vigorous body, and a pure and noble soul, generally refer to man in his second or postnatal state. Religions generally look at man with reference to his third or disembodied state. Systems of Education, of Government, and Religion, have assumed that nothing can be done for human beings, to save them from physical disease and suffering, from vice and crime, and from tendencies to evil, *previous to birth.* Among Ministers of Religion, Legislators, and Rulers; among Poets and Orators, and those who, in all ages and nations, have been received as divinely commissioned and sent to secure to man a healthy body, a strong and comprehensive intellect, a pure and loving heart, a just and noble character, and a happy destiny, and to save the world, no regard has been paid to what is done, or might and must be done for man, for good or evil, before he is born. •

But as soon as he is born, then man becomes an object of interest to parents, teachers, and reformers, and to social, commercial, literary, ecclesiastical, and governmental institutions. The pre-natal state has been ignored, generally, by the family, the school, the college, the pulpit, and the press, and by the Church and State, and regarded as of no account in its bearing on human character and destiny in the post-natal and disembodied states.

In this work I have aimed to show that the period between the conception and birth of human beings, as to the formation of their character and the control of their destiny, after they are born, is the most important period of their existence ; that what is done for them in the pre-natal state, while their organic conditions and tendencies are being formed and fixed, bears more directly and powerfully on their health and happiness of body and soul, than what is done for them after they are born.

The life and happiness of individuals, the love and harmony of families, the prosperity and stability of states and kingdoms, and the protection of life, liberty, and person, are more dependent on influences that bear upon human beings before birth, than on any influence that can be brought to bear on them afterwards. What is *organized* into us in our pre-natal state, is of more consequence to us, and more vital to our triumph over the temptations and obstacles that impede our progress towards perfection and happiness, than what is *educated* into us, after we are born.

THE PRE-NATAL EDUCATION OF MAN! THE MOTHER, THE GOD-APPOINTED EDUCATOR! The one great object of this book is to call attention to these subjects. I do not forget the power of the father in the work of pre-natal education. It cannot be otherwise than great. The impressions made upon the body and soul of the child, through his agency brought to bear on the feelings and sympathies of the mother, must be deep and abiding. But my object is to call attention to the Empire of the Mother, to show the extent of her power, and how it is exerted.

If the ideas put forth in this work be true, they will, in the future, greatly modify the penal codes and establishments and civil governments of the world, and will deeply affect the discipline of children, in families and schools. Humanity will revolt against punishing children for being like their parents, and for being and doing what their parents made them to be and to do. It will be regarded as a wrong and an outrage for parents to organize lying, revenge, cruelty, and every crime into children, and then punish them for acting them out. It will be found to surpass the ingenuity and power of man, to reconcile with love and sympathy for the true and right, the idea of conceiving human beings in sin, and shaping them in iniquity, and predisposing them to evil in their pre-natal state, and then punishing them for being sinners and evil-doers in their post-natal state. An innate sense of justice, and an instinctive reverence for fair dealing, — all that is Divine in Human Nature, will cry out against the practice of organizing theft, robbery, and murder into men before they are born, and then imprisoning or hanging them for becoming thieves, robbers, and murderers after they are born. *Loving discipline*, not *vindictive punishment*, will be the spirit and practice of governments in their dealings with the victims of parental ignorance and outrage.

They, whose organic tendencies are to bodily health and vigor, are not apt to estimate truly the conduct of those whose tendencies are to bodily disease and suffering. They, who are blest with an innate tendency to truth, to honesty, love, forgiveness, and to all purity and nobleness of heart and life, are but ill-qualified to sit in judgment on those who have an inherited tendency to falsehood, dishonesty, wrath, revenge, and to all impurity and viciousness of heart and life. He, in whose soul *upward* tendencies are strong and active, and ever triumphant, can hardly appreciate the struggles of him whose birthright tendencies to drunkenness, to profligacy, and to every degrading and brutalizing passion and habit, predominate over all that is true and noble within him. Pity for the unfortunate will oft touch the heart now filled with indignation for the designedly guilty. The prayer, " Father, forgive them ; they know not what they do," will no longer be merely the prayer of the lips, but the abiding spirit of the heart and life.

If the positions taken in the following pages be true, the Health of Woman, in its bearing on the destiny of the race, will, in the world's future, be regarded as of transcendent importance, and as deserving the special attention of all who seek the elevation and happiness of man, and his progress in all goodness.

But, leaving these subjects to those who are to come after, and who shall earnestly labor, by a war of *ideas*, rather than by a war of *bullets*, to purify and ennoble man, I ask that the positions I have taken be carefully and candidly considered before they are condemned. If they are erroneous, they cannot stand; if true, they cannot be safely neglected. " PROVE ALL THINGS, AND HOLD FAST THAT WHICH " (in your view) " IS GOOD."

HENRY C. WRIGHT.

BOSTON, August 3, 1863.

CONTENTS.

THE EMPIRE OF THE MOTHER.

CHAPTER I.

A MAN OF ONE IDEA.

I am a man of one idea. I have lived for one object, and only for one. What is that one idea so long and so reverently cherished? What that one object so long and earnestly pursued?

THE ELEVATION AND HAPPINESS OF MAN.

This has been my life-long object of pursuit; this, the one controlling idea of my life. In arraying myself against opinions and practices that are consecrated and made venerable by age, and by the character and standing of those who have embraced and pursued them, I have acted with a single eye to this great end; rejecting all opinions and opposing all usages which, in my view, tend to degrade man. Truth can degrade no man. Right can dishonor no man. Whatever is true in principle and right in practice must, of necessity, tend to elevate and ennoble all who adopt and live it. In adopting any new idea or practice, one single thought has controlled me, i. e., Will it tend to purify and ennoble, in myself and others, the nature I bear? Truth

1

and Right must ever produce this result; Error and Wrong cannot.

When it is asked, "What is the chief end of man?" my answer is, and ever has been — to perfect the nature he bears, and to enjoy that perfected nature forever. All my thoughts and feelings, all my plans and purposes, all my interior and exterior life centre in this one idea — THE PERFECTION AND HAPPINESS OF HUMAN NATURE. To ennoble the human type; to develop perfectly all the capabilities of Human Nature; to make man all he is designed to be; and, in this state, to present to the world a more perfect type of manhood and womanhood; to this end it is glorious to live, and gain to die.

It is said — " The chief end of man is to glorify God, and enjoy him forever." My answer is — the only way in which we can glorify God and enjoy him is, to glorify the nature given us, and to be happy in the possession of that glorified nature. To look after the nature we possess, body and soul; to purify and perfect it, and enlarge its capabilities for happiness, and to enjoy that perfected nature; this is the one sole end of our existence, as men and women. I speak to all of human kind; my message is to the race; our sole end of existence is to develop the nature we bear, to its highest possible extent, and make it as beautiful and grand as it is capable of being. In a word, we live but to perfect ourselves, and make ourselves all we are designed to be. Outside of this we can do nothing to glorify and enjoy God. We can add nothing to, nor take from, the richness and majesty of His nature. To refine, beautify, and enjoy ourselves, is to honor and enjoy God in the only sense in which we can honor and enjoy Him.

So far as it is possible for man to harm God, he must do it by harming himself or his fellow-beings; and so far as it is possible for man to do good to God, he must do it by doing good to himself or his fellow-beings. Men and women disgrace God only when they disgrace themselves; they are an honor to God only when they are an honor to themselves. We are true to God's nature only when we are true to our own. We are false to God only when we are false to ourselves. We are infidels to God only when we are infidels to ourselves. In no sense can men and women be a reproach to God, but by being a reproach to themselves. No man can be conscious of God's approval, who is not conscious of his own approval. Man! do thyself no harm, and thou canst do thy God no harm, nor thy fellow-beings. Man's only sin against his God is the sin against himself. He that never sins against himself, can never sin against God.

If we never violate the laws of life and health under which we exist, we can never violate the laws of God. To be obedient to ourselves, is to be obedient to God. Justice and fidelity to man, are justice and fidelity to God. To reverence man, woman and child, is to reverence God. To worship the human is to worship the Divine Nature. Loyalty to ourselves is loyalty to God.

Therefore, I place man first as an object of my aims and efforts. Man is visible and tangible, and his happiness can be increased or diminished by my action. I am a man, and, of necessity, man must be the one ever-present object of thought to me; my affections, aims and actions, inasmuch as they are the affections, aims and actions of a human being, must necessarily centre on human beings, and have reference to their welfare. Man must, of necessity, incarnate God to man as nothing else can. What we do to man we do to God; to wrong ourselves or others is to wrong God; to blaspheme against man is to blaspheme against God; to enslave and

sell man is to enslave and sell God. The true man-wor-
shipper is the true God worshipper.

There are those who devote their powers to perfect the
nature of flowers, fruits and grains, and who feel richly
rewarded by being able to present the most perfect type of
the rose, the apple, or wheat.   Others devote themselves to
the work of perfecting the horse, and of other domestic animals.   This use of human talent is praiseworthy.   It is
laudable to seek to improve and render beautiful and perfect
as possible the surface of the earth, and all the flowers, fruits,
grains, vegetables and animals that are associated with the
existence and happiness of man.   But these are but mere
incidents to human beings.   In themselves they have no significance to us.   They are of value, and it is important and
justifiable to seek to beautify and perfect them, only as they
are thereby made more serviceable to man.   Just so far as
the vegetable and animal kingdoms beneath man, can be
made subservient to his true development and happiness, it is
wise to expend our energies in efforts to improve them.
Minerals, vegetables and animals are of value and deserving
our attention in proportion as they can be made to administer
to the demands of our nature.

So in regard to all efforts made to improve the implements
of agriculture, the means of transporting our persons and
goods, and of conveying our thoughts, affections, and sympathies, around the world ; in regard to efforts designed to make
water, air and electricity work for man to produce and prepare the means to feed and clothe his body, to enlarge and
ennoble his soul, and to supply the demands of his nature
generally, the energies directed to perfect these instrumentalities of human welfare are wisely expended.   But, in themselves, and aside from their relations to human welfare, what
are steam-engines, locomotives, railroads, telegraphs, the

compass, the barometer, the thermometer, chemical apparatus, telescopes, microscopes, books, types, and all other inventions? Nothing; and the efforts expended on them are wasted. Their only value is, in their adaptability to secure to man a nobler and a happier nature and destiny.

There are those, whose energies are devoted to establish, perfect, and administer commercial, literary, social, political, and religious institutions. But what are institutions aside from their relations to man? What are churches, priesthoods, rites and ceremonies; what are schools, colleges and universities; what are governments, constitutions and codes; what are titles, stations and wealth, except as they contribute to the elevation and happiness of human nature? Aside from this, they have no more value than hats and bonnets aside from the heads, shoes aside from the feet, and coats and gowns aside from the bodies which they are designed to benefit; or houses, aside from the human beings for whose comfort and shelter they are built. Harm not the church, the priesthood, the creed; harm not the government, the constitution, the state; harm not the school nor college; harm not society; harm not God; such instructions are urgently and constantly enforced by teachers in church and state. But, "do thyself no harm," and these will take care of themselves.

Not unfrequently those who are loudest in their professions of love for God and regard for his interests and glory, are the very persons who are most open in their manifestations of hatred to men and of hostility to their interests and welfare. Under pretence of a high and sacred regard for God, they are indifferent to the wrongs and sufferings that are inflicted on human beings. But man cannot wrong God except by wronging himself. We cannot rob God except by robbing man. MAN! Be careful never to sin nor blaspheme against thyself nor thy fellow-beings, and thou canst not sin nor blaspheme against God. Never hate thy brother and thou canst not hate God. Despise not nor neglect thy poor and suffering brother, and thou canst never despise nor neglect thy God. Be ever anxious and thoughtful about the comfort the happiness and true glory of the men, women and children that are around thee ; for in this way, alone, canst thou show a true concern for the interests and glory of thy God. " Do I love my neighbor as myself?" Settle this, and thou hast settled the other question, " Do I love God?" For to love man is to love God, in the only practical and profitable way in which we can love him. The knowledge and love of man, in the order of time and in practical value, necessarily precede the love of God. Indeed, we can know and love God only in his manifestations. He who says, "I love God, while he hates his brother, is a liar, and the truth is not in him ; for how can he love God, whom he hath not seen, while he hates his brother whom he hath seen?" Be ever anxious to possess and to show, in all relations, a zeal and readiness to endure scorn, contempt, pain and death, for the good of thy fellow-beings, and in this way alone wilt thou show a beneficent zeal and readiness to suffer and die for God. Whoso suffers rather than inflict suffering on others, and dies rather than kill others, suffers and dies for God, as Jesus did. Let thy whole life be but one sublime, heroic act of love and devotion to thy oppressed, down-trodden and suffering fellow-beings, and in this way alone canst thou worship God in spirit and in truth. *We can know nothing of God except through his manifestations.*

One of the purest spirits ever embodied in human form earnestly and anxiously asks, " Why is nothing ever said about God as being manifest in *living* human beings? Why should we be ever aiming to worship God as an *abstraction?* Why should we not accustom ourselves to see and worship

God in the *living* men, women and children around us?
Especially in the poor, the oppressed and suffering, and in
those who seem most lovable to us, who live in most endearing and intimate relations with us, and whose interests and
happiness would be most essentially promoted by such love
and worship of a manifest God?" Indeed, why should we
not see and worship God in *living* men, women and children?
Let husbands see and worship God in their wives, and wives
in their husbands; parents in their children, and children in
their parents; brothers in sisters, and sisters in brothers; and
let all see and worship God, as Jesus did, in "publicans and
sinners;" in the oppressed, the despised, the outcast and the
suffering. In the language of the person above quoted, "such
love is *God-given* and *God-nourished*. Such worship is *God-
approved* and *God-accepted*, because it identifies the worship
of God with justice, love, kindness, forbearance, gentleness,
patience and long-suffering towards *living* human beings."

Thus let us love and worship God and work and suffer for
God, by loving and respecting our fellow-beings, and by
laboring and suffering, to elevate and ennoble them, and make
them good and happy, and we shall surely hear the welcome
— "Come, thou blessed of the Father, enter into the kingdom prepared for thee; for, inasmuch as thou hast done it
unto these my brethren, thou hast done it unto me." Those
who think of God and seek to glorify God, aside from man;
who, under pretence of being swallowed up in God, overlook
their fellow-beings, and pass by those who have fallen among
thieves, may pride themselves on their zeal for God; but
they are strangers to that spirit which leads to doing good,
and makes it "more blessed to give than receive;" which
thinketh and doeth no evil, and which is all-hoping, all-trusting, all-forgiving, and all-enduring. Having no zeal for
man, they can have none for God.

Man, then, is my one idea ; his perfection and happiness my one object. To beautify and ennoble the nature I bear is worthy the entire consecration of all my powers. All other ideas and objects are, in my view, secondary to this. We can never estimate too highly our nature and our destiny. Man is, indeed, clothed with majesty as with a garment ; a crown of glory is on his head ; a diadem of beauty encircles his brow, placed there by the Eternal. All things are placed beneath his feet, and his dominion is over all, secondary and subject only to that great, vitalizing, all-controlling Power in whom we live, move and have our being, and who is made visible and tangible most perfectly in man, and who can be truly and acceptably worshipped by us only in deeds of love and justice to our fellow-beings. Man's whole duty is summed up in one short sentence : LOYALTY TO HIS OWN NATURE. Man owes allegiance to nothing in the universe whose existence necessarily conflicts with the perfection and happiness of a single human being. Fear thyself, and fear nothing else. *Self-respect* is the only basis of respect for others. Reverence thyself, and be not troubled about respecting any being or power outside of thyself.

Do THYSELF NO HARM. — This comprises the whole of life and duty. He who does himself no harm, can do God no harm. He who does himself no harm, can do his fellow-beings no harm. Indeed, man can do no harm to God ; he has power only to harm himself and his fellow-beings. As to what is harmful to us, each must judge for himself ; but whatever a man judges to be hurtful to himself, he decides to be hurtful to others. He that says another is a villain who attempts to enslave him, decides that he himself is a villain when he enslaves, or apologizes for enslaving, another. He who would shoot another who should attempt to enslave his wife and children, decides that he himself ought to be shot when, by his vote or otherwise, he enslaves the wives and children of others.   So in all things; whatever is hurtful to us, we being judges, we know is hurtful to others when we do it to them; and he is " a liar, and the truth is not in him," who pretends to love and worship God, while he does to others that which he is not willing others should do to him; and who does or apologizes for doing to others what he would count an insult, a disgrace, and an outrage when done to him.

So what a man decides to be wrong or blasphemous when done to God, he decides to be wrong or blasphemous when done to man.   Whatever is a sin and a blasphemy against God, is a sin and blasphemy against man.   He who has no respect for man, has none for God.   No man can worship God, while he scorns the poorest and humblest of his children — for in every man, woman and child, God " is made flesh, to dwell among us," to be loved and worshipped by us. Thus I associate man, not his incidents and appendages, with what I hold most sacred, and would labor to make him worthy to be thus intimately associated with my highest conception of the true, the just, the loving, and the good.

1*

CHAPTER II.

MAN THE RESULT OF HUMAN AGENCY.

HUMAN BEINGS may be viewed from two stand-points ; i. e. (1.) Divine Agency.   (2.) Human Agency.   As seen from the former, man, as to existence, organization, character and destiny, is regarded as the workmanship of God ; as seen from the latter, he is considered the workmanship of man. There are two theories or systems of philosophy and religion ; one regards and deals with man as the result of Divine, the other as the result of Human Agency.

In all practical efforts to elevate and perfect the nature we bear, success depends essentially on which of these two theories we adopt.   Those who consider man as the result of divine agency, will pursue a course very different from the one adopted by those who regard him as the result of human agency.   Those who regard slavery as the result of divine agency, will deal with it, and those who practise it, in a manner widely different from that which will be adopted by those who regard it as the result of human agency.

Is man the effect of a cause over which we have any control?   If he is not, we can never improve the result by improving the cause — for the cause is above and beyond our reach ; no efforts of ours can change the nature and operations of the antecedent.   If the fountain, whence our organic existence, character and destiny are derived, is beyond our reach, and can, in no way, be affected by our efforts, we can exercise no control over the effect by seeking to change the character of the cause. But if we can, to any extent, control the conditions of the fountain, we can, by purifying and improving those conditions, purify the streams that flow from it.

There is a lake. Many streams flow from it. Can human agency control the conditions of that lake? Can its waters be made sweeter or more bitter, more clear or more muddy, more wholesome or unwholesome, by our efforts? If so, then can we, by changing the conditions of the lake, change the conditions of the streams flowing from it. Human agency can decide whether those streams shall be sweet or bitter, wholesome or unwholesome. But if we have no control over the conditions of the lake, we cannot, through the fountain change the character and direction of the streams. We may work at the streams, and succeed in making them purer for a moment, but the impure waters of the lake are, without ceasing, being poured into these streams, and no progress can be made in permanently improving them while the fountain from which they flow is turbid and poisonous. So long as the lake is a cesspool of corruption, no power can render the streams clear and wholesome.

So in regard to human beings: if the fountain from which they derive organic life, be filled with disease, that life must also be diseased. And if human agency can exert no influence over the conditions of that fountain, it cannot affect the character of the streams that come from it. If we can purify the source, we can the individual men and women that come from it. Can we control the existence, organization, character and destiny of man, by purifying the fountain of his organic life, or must we settle down in the conviction that man is the result of an agency over which we can exercise no control?

In all my efforts to improve and perfect the human type, I view men and women from the stand-point of human agency — solely. So far as they are the result of a divine agency, I have no power to improve them. God is beyond my control; I cannot improve his nature, nor change his conditions, for better or for worse. He must and will perfect his own work. He does not wish us to enter into his field of labor. He will attend to his own affairs, and, so far as our elevation and happiness depend on his agency, the work will be done, and well done. No interference of ours can make the least change in him, as to his plans, his feelings, his motives, his exertions, or as to the times and means of his accomplishing his work.

But what man can make, man can mar or mend. What human agency can create, the same can improve. So far as the human organism is the result of human agency, this same power can mar or mend it, — can obstruct or perfect its action, — can bring to it health or disease, happiness or misery. As he that can make a watch, or a locomotive, can take it to pieces, and put it together, can obstruct or facilitate its operations, so is it with the human organism; so far as its existence, character, and destiny result from human agency, we can beautify or deform it, we can control its functions, and obstruct or perfect their action. But so far as that organism, including soul and body, is the result of divine agency, a power over which we can never exercise control, and so far as its operations depend upon that, God alone can regulate its movements; and, if obstructions impede its healthy action, in any or in all of its functions, we must look to God alone to remove them.

Consequently, that theory or system of anthropology, (the only true theology,) which regards the human organism as the result of divine agency, directs us to look to the same power to remove the obstacles that impede its perfect action. If it becomes diseased, by any means, and its action becomes deranged and suffering ensues, God is supposed to be the only power that can remove the disease, and restore the system to healthy action. If scrofula, consumption, cancer, fever, dyspepsia, small-pox, or any disease gets into that organism, the assumption is, that the Being, on whose agency its existence and healthy action depend, can alone remove the disease and restore it to its normal conditions. So of diseases of the soul, by which its healthful and happy action is deranged; anger, hatred, revenge, ambition, avarice, jealousy, envy, and the many appetites and passions that afflict our souls, and utterly derange them in their relations to others; as these conditions of the soul, so discordant and foreign to their true life, are supposed to be the result of a power outside of man and above human control, so all religions teach us to look to a recuperative power aside from human agency.

So of war, drunkenness, slaveholding, murder, piracy, polygamy, robbery and anarchy, — these, especially slavery, that comprises them all, and is the " sum of *all* villany," are supposed to be the result of an agency above human control, and men are taught to wait patiently God's time to remove them.

How to induce God to remove these diseases of body and soul, and to restore the deranged functions of our physical, social and moral nature to healthful and harmonious action? is the one great question of all religions. God is supposed to be angry with us, and, as an expression of his hot wrath, sends upon us these diseases. How to appease his anger and get him into such a state of feeling towards us that he shall be willing to cleanse our bodies and souls from their diseases and save us from the sufferings that afflict us? This is what all religions aim to show.

All religions, of the past and present, propose essentially the same means to avert the wrath of God and to induce him to exert his power to heal and save. Some external rites, ceremonies, or sacrifices are prescribed. Fruits and products of the earth are offered ; prayers and fastings, or the sacrifice of some appetite or passion, or pleasure ; the sacrifice of animals, or of a human being, and outward acts of worship, — these have been prescribed by all religions. It is supposed that the heart of God can be moved to pity, and induced, by such outward sacrifices, to heal our diseases of body and soul, and assuage our pains and sorrows resulting from them, and rescue us from hell and raise us to heaven ; or, what is the same, to take away disease from the human organism and give it health.

And even while praying and laboring to induce God to exert his power to heal them, they do the very things which they know will derange their systems and produce disease and suffering. They pray God to save them from the poverty, the diseases, the anguish, the delirium tremens, and the premature death, the idiocy, the insanity and crimes, resulting from the use of alcohol and tobacco, and at the same time use these poisons. They pray and labor to induce God to save them and their country from the results of war and slavery, while they, at the same time, justify and practise these deeds of blood and violence. They pray God to save themselves and families from licentiousness, and at the same time, live in prostitution, licensed or unlicensed, or both. While they pray God to save them from anger, wrath, revenge, evil-speaking, envy, jealousy, covetousness and ambition, they cherish, justify and strengthen these passions. They pray to be saved from headache, dyspepsia, consumption, rheumatism, and fever, yet habitually indulge in the very habits and practices which, they know, will introduce and strengthen these diseases within them. They pray God to save their children from scrofula, cancer, erysipelas, and all inherited diseases, and to bestow on them healthy bodies and souls ; yet, so live in their domestic relations, as to entail on them diseased and vicious tendencies. They pray God to spare the lives of their children, yet so live as to entail on them premature death. Thus while they appeal to God's agency to preserve them and theirs in health and life, they exert their own agency to inflict on themselves and their offspring disease and death. While they trust in and look to God to raise them up to heaven, they put forth their own energies in efforts to plunge themselves and their children into hell.

Such is the result of a theory, or system, which regards the existence, organization, character and destiny of man, as the result of divine agency. If more children are born to parents than they can support and properly care for, their existence is attributed to God, and it is considered all his doing and marvellous in their eyes. In the existence of children, and in their organic and constitutional birthright tendencies, human agency is supposed to have no concern. If an unwelcome child is born, whose existence is repulsive to both parents, still, because it is supposed to exist by Divine agency, and in accordance with the will of God, therefore they are urged to submit quietly to the inscrutable doings of a wise Providence.

If a human being is born, and that living organism is made up of the worst possible materials, and those diseased and imperfect materials are most imperfectly put together, so that there is no soundness in it, it is assumed that these materials were selected and made up into that deformed and suffering organism by Divine agency ; and the parents of such a child are exhorted to be still, and recognize, in the diseases and agonies of their child, the work of a kind but mysterious Providence. And when that diseased and suffering body dies, the parents are again told to be still, and know that it is God that afflicts them, and to kiss the rod that smites them.

So when our domestic, social, ecclesiastical, political and commercial relations and associations become corrupt and inharmonious, as the result of the diseases and discords that afflict the bodies and souls of individuals, such corruptions and discords are supposed to result from an agency over which we have no control. Human agency, as connected with their existence or removal, is ignored. Consequently, all efforts to heal these diseases and inharmonies of families, and social, religious, and political combinations, are made with reference to this supposed fact, that God gave them, and God must take them away; that an outside God sends coldness, indifference, hatred and contentions into families, and that the same power must remove them; that God gets up malignant and murderous quarrels in churches, and that God must put them down; and that he may be induced to do so by much praying and fasting; that God gives war, slavery, drunkenness, rapine, insurrections, rebellions, and all the horrors of anarchy, and God must take them away, and our work is to bless him whether he gives or takes. Thus, those who view man as the result of Divine agency, as to his existence, organization, character and destiny, wait upon the Lord, and do nothing themselves, except, it may be, to apologize for and practise the very evils they want God to remove.

A FOREST SCENE. — Several years past, I took part in a convention called to consider the following question: *What shall we do to be saved?* The scene was a forest. Many hundreds assembled. A grand and glorious forest of great extent encircled that great gathering. Of all subjects which, in the dead past or the living present, have occupied human thoughts, awakened human sympathy and anxiety, and called into intense activity human energy, this has been the most prominent and important. For what else do religions exist with their array of priesthoods and churches, their prayers, fastings and sacrifices, their rites and ceremonies, and their holy times, places and creeds, but to answer this one great inquiry? For what do governments exist, with their constitutions and codes, their array of legislators, judges and executives, and of penal and military establishments, their armies and navies, and penitentiaries and gallows, but to solve this simplest, most intelligible, yet most mysterious and bewildering of all human problems? No question is so fraught with human character and destiny as this. Well may men and women gather, in anxious crowds, beneath the overshadowing forests and vaulted sky, and there, on God's great anxious seat, ask — *What shall we do to be saved?*

At this convention, all of every class of religionists were present by public invitation. The question was propounded in due form, and we were all invited to give, each, such an answer as his convictions prompted. Substantially the same answer was given by all till I was invited to give one. I came upon the platform and said.—"Before giving my opinion on the question before the meeting, I would like to ask and briefly answer two other questions, i. e. : (1.) Who is responsible for the existence of children? (2.) Who is responsible for their organization?" Leave being granted, I said—"The first question in the children's catechism, is— 'Child! Who made you?' Answer—'God.' This is false, as every child understands it ; this being the impression made and designed to be made, *that God is responsible for the existence of children.* The answer releases the parents from responsibility, and places it upon an agency aside from human. Whereas, parents know that it is as false to say that God is responsible for the existence of their children, as it would be to hold God responsible for the death of a man who cuts his own throat. You steal a woman and enslave her ; and your child asks — ' Who made that woman a slave?' and you answer — ' God.' You hang a man, and your child asks — ' Who hung that man?' and you answer — ' God.' You bombard and burn a city, and your child asks — ' Who burnt that city?' You say — ' God.' A man drinks rum and gets drunk, and the child asks — ' Who made him a drunkard?' and you say — ' God.' Do you not know this is a falsehood? But the existence of children is no less the result of human agency ; and men and women are as really responsible for the results of their voluntary acts in one case as in the other. Yet, parents persist in teaching their children, as the basis of a religious education, that God is responsible for their existence. Yet they all know that God is no more responsible for the existence of children, than he is for the death of the man that the state hangs, or for the enslavement of the woman that is sold by the kidnapper."

The assembly was greatly agitated. A woman who, with her husband, sat before me, arose and said in great excitement — " Do you mean to tell me that God is not the father of my children?" " But my friend," I said, " I had hitherto supposed that the man who sits by you was the father of your children, and I think you would be shocked and offended if I or any other should say he was not." She dropped into her seat and said no more. A minister then arose and said — " Mr. Wright, if I understand you, you deny the doctrine of *regeneration*, do you not?" " Why, my good man," said I, " if you had been rightly *generated*, you would not have needed to be *re-generated*, would you?" He sat down to digest an idea that had evidently never entered his mind before. " It is far better," I continued, " more natural, more economical and more divine, to expel disease from, and restore health to the human organism, and to save the race from crime and woe by *generation* than by *regeneration*. Give to children, as a birthright inheritance, healthy and vigorous bodies, and pure and noble souls, and the world's huge, expensive, clumsy and most inefficient apparatus of regeneration, might, for most part, be laid aside. The ecclesiastical establishments of mankind would have nothing to do."

Another minister rose and said — " Mr. Wright, you deny that we must be born of God in order to inherit the kingdom of heaven, do you not?" " Why, man," I said, " had you been rightly and healthfully born of *woman*, there had been no need that you should be born of God afterwards, would there? To be born of woman, the offspring of love, and with a healthy body and soul, is to be born of God. The child of love is the true child of God. Those who are born with healthy bodies and pure souls, are born of God, and enter into the kingdom of heaven at the outset of life. It is far easier to keep right after we are started right, than to get right after we have been started wrong. There is far more reason to hope that those, who are born with healthy and pure organisms, will retain their innate health and purity, than that those who are born to the sad inheritance of diseased bodies and souls, should ever attain to a pure and healthy organism. Better, far better, that the mother should introduce her child into the kingdom of heaven at its natural birth, than to be brought into it by some artificial birth, produced by the church, after running a course of sin and degradation." This minister sat down to ponder, in silence, an idea which evidently seemed to him very natural and replete with good sense, but which had never before been brought home to his reason and conscience. The thoughts and feelings of that whole convention seemed to receive a new direction, and the conviction to be deep and lasting that human agency had very much to do with the human organism, not only as to its existence, but also as to the diseased or healthful, the painful or pleasurable action of its powers and functions.

It is asked — Shall we entirely ignore the agency of God in the propagation, perpetuation, perfection and happiness of the human organism? This we cannot do; every breath we draw, every pulsation of the heart, every thought and feeling, every power and function of this living organism, is an ever-present testimony to each one, that there is an agency concerned in the existence, development, and happiness of human beings, which is above and beyond all human control, and which is the vitalizing, impelling, elevating and ennobling power of human nature. Yet, while conscious of the existence and presence of that power in all vegetable and animal life, we cannot ignore the fact, that the existence of each and every human organism is the result of a voluntary relation on the part of the parents; and that the conditions of that organism and its character and destiny, must essentially depend on the conditions of the parents, and especially of the mother.

CHAPTER III.

OUR SAVIOUR IS BORN WITH US.

IN all my efforts to perfect the type of manhood and womanhood, to expel disease from the human organism and make it more healthy and happy in all its functions, I view man solely from the stand-point of human agency; of SELF-REDEMPTION. I assume that man can and must " work out his own salvation," or he never will be saved. I regard his organic existence, his pre-natal and post-natal development, and his character and destiny, as they are controlled and modified by the power and influence of men and women.

The living human organism is before me. I see it and recognize its existence and presence in myself, and in all my fellow-beings around me. That organism is made up of different elements. Of all species of mechanism, natural or artificial, divine or human, this seems the most delicate, most complicated, the most simple, yet most mysterious and wonderful; and that with which I have most to do; and with which my life and destiny are most intimately associated. Its beauty, its strength, its health, its endurance, and the symmetry, harmony and perfection of all its parts and operations, can never with impunity be undervalued, nor in any way neglected; for on these are based the life, the glory and destiny of the human race. Every thing relating to the history of that organism, relates to me. Its history is my history, its existence, growth, diseases and sufferings are mine. All that adorns and ennobles it adorns and ennobles me ; all that deforms and degrades it deforms and degrades me. Whatever is done to man is done to me. He that enslaves any human being, however poor and despised, enslaves me, and I shall ever regard and treat him, in the same way in which I should, were I the victim of his injustice and inhumanity.

By human organism, I mean a human being, with all the powers and attributes that are necessary to constitute a human being. In this phrase, I include whatever is necessary to make a man or woman, physically, intellectually, socially and spiritually; all that is included in the words human body and soul. Whatever causes deformity and suffering to this organism, whatever disturbs and renders imperfect and painful its action in any of its functions, I designate by the words disease, injury, deformity or abnormal action.

As I view this organism and examine into its interior conditions, and the operations of its various functions, I notice some facts respecting it which are as visible and undisputed as is the fact of its existence. Of which are the following : —

(1.) This organism is diseased, i. e., its functions in many respects are deranged, its action is irregular, discordant and painful.

(2.) These diseases or deformities, or deranged and painful operations, are the result of human agency, directly or indirectly, voluntary or involuntarily, ignorantly or knowingly exerted.

(3.) These diseases can be cured only by human agency, i. e., by the voluntary or involuntary, the conscious or unconscious action of a power within the organism itself. The power to cure disease and redeem from suffering is within. If cured and saved at all, man must be self-cured and self-redeemed.

Thus viewing the diseases of the human organism as the result of human agency, and looking to the same power or agency to effect the cure, I direct my energies accordingly; and base my efforts on the fact, that here is a work that must be done, and that man must do it or it never will be done; that no external agency can ever improve the nature we bear, and if that nature is ever to be developed into a nobler type of manhood or womanhood, it must be done by the "Saviour that is born in us and with us." The soul of each man or woman is the only manger in which his or her Messiah can be born.

In this I plan and act as I do in other matters pertaining to daily life. If my watch is irregular or in any way obstructed or deranged in its operations, if a screw is loose, if a chain or spring is broken, if a cog or wheel is bent or loose so that the action of the watch is imperfect, and it ceases to answer the end of its existence, i. e., to note correctly the passing of time, I go to the same power that made it to repair it. If the locomotive is obstructed in its action and fails to answer the end for which it was made, we go to the person that made it to mend it. If the organ is out of tune, we resort to the power that made it to mend it. So in regard to the diseases that affect the human organism; the power that produces them must cure them.

But it may be asked, may not the power that introduces disease into the system be unable to cast it out? Undoubtedly; the mother may organize scrofula, consumption, dyspepsia, or neuralgia into her child and have no power to cast it out. By the use of tobacco, alcohol and other poisons, human beings may bring into their systems various and painful diseases, and have no power to heal them. What then? If the disease be in the body, the patient must suffer until through suffering he " ceases to do evil and learns to do well."

It is asked, is it not true, after all, that we must fall back upon the divine agency for healing and salvation? Certain it is that, if a human organism or being, is wounded or in any way diseased, no external applications can heal that wound. When the body is injured by any means, no outward medicine can ever repair the injury. The recuperator or redeemer is in that material organism. Outward applications may remove obstacles to the effectual and speedy action of that vital force or recuperator, but they cannot expel the disease, heal the wound, join the fractured bones, or restore healthy and vigorous action to the injured bodily organs and functions. No drugs, nor outward appliances, can purify or cleanse the blood from the corrupt and diseased matter that lurks within it. All this must be done by that inward power or sentinel, whose business it is to watch over the life and health of the body, to keep all enemies from entering it, as far as possible, and drive them out if they have gained entrance. A redeemer is organized into each body as its birthright inheritance.

So of the soul, or the intellectual, social and spiritual part of that living organism, called man or woman. If, by any means, it becomes deranged in any of its functions; if it becomes wounded, by harboring in it envy, jealousy, anger, wrath, revenge, ambition, avarice, or by any outward demonstrations of these passions, no power outside of that soul, with any outward appliances, can possibly heal these diseases, expel these enemies of its peace and happiness, and restore it to healthy, harmonious action in its various powers and functions. The laws of the soul are violated if love, justice, truth, purity, benevolence, forgiveness, self-denial, self-sacrifice, which are as essential to the life and health of the soul as food, air and sleep are to the body, are outraged. The natural action of the soul is deranged, and suffering and anguish must ensue. The recuperator or redeemer to heal that soul, and restore it to health and heaven, is within itself, as a part and parcel of its existence. It is the birthright inheritance of every soul, as well as of every body, and can never die, nor become inoperative while the soul lives. It is Nature's sentinel, set to watch the soul, that no enemy enter its sacred enclosure, or, if it has entered, to drive it out and destroy it.

Thus there is in every human being or organism, a recuperator, or saviour. Call it God, or Divine agency, if we will; but whatever it is called, it is an essential element of human nature, and can never be disregarded in our estimate of man, and in our efforts to cure his diseases and give to him health and vigor. This recuperative power is as essential a part of every human organism, as is love, reason, or will. What it does, is done by human agency, as really as if done by visible hands and fingers. Call it God, if thou wilt, but it is God so blended with man, that they cannot be separated. The action of the God, in healing and saving the soul or body, is the action of the man. The action of the Divine is also the action of the human agent. Though it may be said that, in all our efforts to elevate and glorify the Nature we bear, it is God who must work in us, prompting us to will and to do, yet my position is true, that "Man must work out his own salvation," if he is ever saved. Man, not God, must "cease to do evil, and learn to do well," or the heaven of innocence and love can never enter his soul.

In a London Medical College, a number of students were being examined with a view to obtain diplomas. To one student, the examining professor put this question : "Will you give a concise definition of the Healing Art?" "THE ART OF AMUSING THE PATIENT WHILE NATURE CURES THE

DISEASE," was the answer. A truer and more comprehensive answer was never given to that question. The Healing Art! The art of expelling disease from, and restoring health to, the entire human organism, body and soul. The art of saving man, or of restoring harmonious action to all the powers and functions of his physical, intellectual, domestic, social and spiritual nature and relations; the art of elevating men and women, as individuals, as families, as societies, states, and nations, from a hell-state into a heaven-state! What is it? Simply the art of removing obstructions to health, while Nature cures the disease. Cease to do evil, cease to repeat the injury, while Nature, or the God within us, heals the wounds already made. No power in the universe can heal the human organism of its wounds, while those wounds are being repeated. No power can save a man from drunkenness, lying, sensualism, hatred, slaveholding, murder, piracy, or any wrong, while he persists in the practice of these outrages on himself and others. No power can raise a soul to heaven while it persists in plunging into hell. "Cease to do evil, and do well," and Nature, or the Saviour within, will heal the wounds already made.

The human being, then, or organism, is to be healed of all diseases, not by an external power, but by the balm and physician that are born with and in that organism, as essential elements of its existence. Exterior agents may help on the cure by removing obstacles, but the inborn redeemer must do the work, and restore the system, body and soul, to perfect and healthy action. The power within must place the organism in a condition of harmony with itself, in all its functions, and with all other human organisms, and with every being and thing in the universe.

It will be asked, " What of the doctrine that there is no recuperator, no power to expel disease, and restore health, to save from hell and raise to heaven, within any human organism? That each and every human being is without any recuperator or redeeming power, in himself or herself, and must depend solely on an external power to cure his or her diseases, and restore him or her, to health and happiness of body and soul?" I say that it is simply false; because opposed to the testimony and facts of human and of universal nature. There is no power in one tree to heal the wounds given to another; no power in one animal to heal the injuries inflicted on another animal; no power in one human body to heal the wounds and cast out the diseases inflicted on another human body. The life-principle or God-element in each tree, animal or human body, must perform the cure of all injuries and diseases inflicted on that tree, animal or body. Thus far all admit the fact, that the recuperator, or redeemer within us, must do the work. All that can be done by any outward agency, is, to remove obstacles to the free, natural, and speedy action of the saviour within.

But when we come to the soul or psychical part of the man, the existence of a birthright recuperator or redeemer, is ignored, and an external physician or recuperator, is introduced, as the only power that can cure the diseases and deformities of that. It is admitted that every thing that has vegetable or animal life, except the soul of man, is favored with an ever-present, ever-watchful, ever-active, innate recuperator or redeemer, fully competent to heal all injuries that are curable; but when we come to this, the noblest manifestation of power and wisdom, on this planet, no innate redeemer is provided; but the human soul must look beyond itself, and trust to the chance of finding some external arbitrary power, to heal its diseases.

I shall assume that human souls are to be cured of their diseases and sufferings and restored to health and happiness

— are to be purified, ennobled and saved by the same process by which human bodies are to be healed. I shall assume that there is, in each soul, a power all-sufficient to make it just what it was designed to be, and all it is capable of being, and to place it, ultimately, in harmonious and happy relations with all other souls and with God. The sole business of practical reformers or redeemers is, to remove all obstacles to the vigorous action of the innate, birthright saviour — that it may bring its energies all to bear on the great work of inducing the ignorant, mistaken man or woman to " cease to do evil and learn to do well " — that the redemption of the soul may be perfectly wrought out, and made complete in righteousness and be filled with all the fulness of love and of God.

I wound a tree. The recuperator within instantly goes to work to heal the wound. But, if I keep repeating the wound, no cure can be performed. I cut my finger; the recuperator or saviour born in and with my body, instantly goes to work to repair the injury. But the only condition of success is, that I cease to repeat the wound. No power within or without the body can ever effect a cure if I continue to repeat the wound. So of the soul; I wound it; instantly that recuperator, saviour or redeemer, that was born with and in my soul, rallies to drive out the enemy, to heal the wound, and restore health and soundness to it. But, I repeat the injury, and keep repeating it, and thus render all efforts to heal and to save my soul ineffectual. No God, no Christ, whether within or without, — no church, no state, no priests, nor politicians, no creeds nor constitutions, no prayers nor tears, can ever redeem my soul, except on condition that I " cease to do evil and learn to do well." Ceasing to do evil and learning to do well, is redemption in the only sense in which it can practically be ours. The more perfectly our souls are endowed with an organic, constitutional tendency to good, the more potent will be this inborn saviour to save us.

Man has, then, within himself a saviour, born with and in him. This saviour, or redeemer, or God within us, is ever saying to us — Do THYSELF NO HARM! And if through ignorance or other cause we do harm ourselves in body or soul, this inborn Jesus, this birth-right saviour, is ever saying to us — " Come to me, take my yoke upon thee, and thou shalt find rest." What yoke? This, and this only: CEASE TO DO EVIL — LEARN TO DO WELL.

CHAPTER IV.

PHYSICAL DESTINY FIXED BY ORGANIZATION.

THE Human Race is a Unit. We are alike in the general features and attributes of body and soul. The bones, nerves, muscles, and membranes of all, are alike in their structure, location, action and uses. We are alike in the general structure and tendencies of our souls. All are under similar laws, having similar wants, a similar origin, common sympathies and a common destiny. Such is the likeness, that a human being can be instantly distinguished from every other animal. Yet no two are alike ; each individual having something that serves to distinguish him from each and every other. In the color and expression of the eyes ; in the form and expression of the countenance ; in the tones of the voice ; in all the manifestations of will, reason, affection, sympathy and conscience, and in all outward demonstrations of intellect and affection, there is something which enables us to distinguish one from another. We are warranted in the conclusion that — *Nature never repeats herself ;* but, in each one, presents a new type of manhood or womanhood. While each has all the general elements and attributes that distinguish the human being from every other species of animal, there is a something in the form and manifestations of each, that serves to give to him or her a marked individuality.

All have reason, but in each, reason differs in degree and direction ; all have power to love and sympathize, yet in each it differs in depth, in earnestness, in endurance and direction. All have will, but in each, how different its manifestations! All have veneration and conscience, but how different their direction and manifestations in each! The conscience of one directing him to do that which that of another directs him to condemn. The conscience of a Christian and of a Mohammedan, of an abolitionist and a slaveholder, of the self-abnegationist and the self-preservationist; how different in its direction and its susceptibility!

Whence this difference? There is a natural cause that is subject to human observation, and, to some extent, to human control. Why is one healthy and another diseased — one hopeful and another desponding — one cheerful and another melancholy — one generous and another ungenerous — one suspicious and another confiding — one noble and another ignoble — one happy and another unhappy? Why is one revengeful and another forgiving — one loving and lovable, and another unloving and unlovable — one honest and another dishonest — one selfish and another unselfish? Why is one abandoned to theft, drunkenness, licentiousness, violence and murder, and another incapable of being tempted to commit these crimes? Why has one great power to resist the influence of deleterious and debasing material, social and moral surroundings, and another no power? Why is one a Jesus of Nazareth, and another a slave-hunter or a pirate?

Behold the pestilence that walketh in darkness — the destruction that wastes at noon-day! In the same family, one is taken and the others left. In neighborhoods and towns, here and there, one is taken and others left. Side by side lie the dead bodies of the infant of a day and of the man of seventy, and by them lie the bodies of the maiden of sixteen and the matron of sixty. Why is this? Is the cause in the outward surroundings, or in a defective internal structure? The diseased surroundings that lay many physical human organisms in the dust, have no power at all over others; solely, because some have more innate power to resist them than others, and because a tendency to imbibe disease is stronger in some than in others.

Go visit yon School, Academy, or College; observe the difference in the strength, aptitude, and manifestations of intellect. Go to yon play-ground; observe the variety in the tempers, dispositions, passions and propensities of the jubilant group there assembled. Their untamed hearts and exuberant spirits, all shout out the great chorus of Humanity, yet how various their modes of manifestation. How each differs from each and every other in character and destiny. One is rough, another polished; one gentle, another ungentle; one is loud and boisterous, another quiet and peaceful; one obtrusive, another unobtrusive; one is irritable or sulky, or revengeful, another calm, self-possessed, kindly forbearing, and forgiving.

Whence this difference in the character and destiny of human beings? Where must we look for the force or influence that gives character to their thoughts and feelings, their appetites and passions, their plans and actions, and that issues in such different results in individuals, who in general characteristics are so much alike? Whence the difference in the daily and hourly destiny of each? Is it caused by an interior or exterior force? Is it to be found in the innate, internal structure and development of each individual organism; or in the material, intellectual, social and spiritual surroundings? Is it a power over which the individual has a conscious, voluntary control, or one whose influence is ever-present, ever-felt, and ever-potent for good or evil, but before which the individual soul is powerless? Is the power that thus controls the manifestations of intellect, affection, passion, appetite and the interior and exterior action and life of the entire organism, constitutional and organic — or is it adventitious and educational? Behold the revelations and manifestations of the living human organisim, in all their varieties and ramifications in agriculture, mechanics, commerce, science, literature, art, in all domestic, social, religious, political and commercial relations — in war, slavery, drunkenness, and every species of crime and immorality! Is the power that produces these results, so various, so diverse and complicated, within or without that living, human mechanism?

Passing by the nursery, the family, the school, the church, the state, conventionalism, and all other material, social, religious, civil, intellectual, exterior surroundings, I would direct attention to the organization itself, and say —

As is the Organization — so will be the character and destiny of the individual man or woman and of the race.

By organism or organization, I mean the whole man or woman — including soul as well as body. The soul, I shall assume, without argument, is an organized structure as well as the body; and has organic conditions and tendencies; an organism within an organism, the former being the vitalizing, motive power of the latter; a kingdom within a kingdom, the former combining, adjusting, directing and ruling the latter. The former is the *psychical*, the latter the *physical* kingdom. Both harmoniously blended, make the united kingdom of God and man — the body being the kingdom of God, as truly as the soul.

Is it a truth, a simple fact of human life, that as is the organization, so will be the character and destiny of the individual? Or, in other words — Is destiny determined by organization? Is the action, or manifestation of the soul,

2*

of the man or woman determined by organic conditions and constitutional tendencies?

In pursuing this inquiry two questions arise. (1.) Are human character and destiny at all affected by organization? (2.) If so, to what extent?

That our character and happiness are affected, more or less, by organic conditions and tendencies, is attested by the experience of each and every one. It is simply a matter of consciousness, a self-evident truth, which no argument can refute or confirm, nor make more intelligible. As to the extent of that influence, opinions vary — some affirming that human organisms or beings have absolutely no more control over their interior or exterior actions and manifestations, than has a clock or locomotive; and others, that within the limits of fixed and beneficent laws, they can and do control their destiny.

Consider the organic conditions of the body. What influence do these, daily and hourly, have on the interior and exterior life and happiness? Do they have any? The life of each man or woman is a fact, demonstrating that the character and destiny of each one are momentarily and essentially affected by such conditions; that the intellectual, affectional and passional manifestations of the soul depend, essentially, on the organic conditions of the body. Certain conditions of the body predispose to headache. What those conditions are, we may not be able to tell precisely; yet we know that headache and freedom from that pain cannot result from the same physical conditions. The same cause cannot produce effects so dissimilar; the same tree cannot produce fruit so unlike and contradictory. Mothers, subject to headaches, seldom fail to organize into their children, a tendency to the same, so that whatever affects the digestion or the nerves unfavorably, ends in this disease. Certain organic bodily conditions necessarily result in the suffering called dyspepsia. Though we may not, in our present ignorance be able to determine what are those conditions that result in this kind of suffering, yet we do know that the pain and the absence of it, cannot result from the same organic conditions. Mothers affected by this disease, seldom fail to organize it into their children. So cancer, scrofula, and consumption, are generally the results of certain organic physical conditions and tendencies. The pain and suffering designated by these words, must of necessity, always result from similar bodily conditions.

We may not, in the present state of our knowledge in regard to human physiology, be able to say what conditions will necessarily produce these sad and painful effects; yet, we do know that they must be different from those which produce opposite results. The fact that a man has those conditions which must of necessity result in such sufferings, can, as yet, be known only by the fact, that the results exist. Will knowledge ever be so increased, that the conditions may be known independent of the results? That we may know before the results appear, that such and such bodies will surely be affected by such and such diseases? So of all physical diseases and sufferings, resulting from organic conditions; we know there is a defect in the system somewhere, or these results would never be experienced. The consciousness of the pain demonstrates the existence of a defect in the system.

Physical disease and death may result from causes that are not organic. They may be produced by external causes. So far as the particular disease or suffering is concerned, the organic conditions may be sound and productive of conscious joy. These conditions may be such that existence, in itself, may be conscious and uninterrupted bliss, a succession of exulting sensations. Every throb of the heart, every bounding pulse may be heaven. Yet, exterior influences may bear upon us, to produce disease and pain, and entirely defeat the end of those healthful, happy, organic conditions. The organic action may be perfect in itself, and yet the individual destiny be made most painful, through external surroundings. But the diseased conditions of material surroundings, may be and often are resisted by a superior, internal power, that protect the body from their influence. But this vital energy or force must be organized into that body, before birth, or it can hardly be created afterwards, by any process of outward discipline. The power, or ability to resist must be there, or no resistance can be made. No one can exert forces that he does not possess.

It is within the certain knowledge of every one, that the above-named diseases and others, and the sufferings and deaths resulting from them, not unfrequently, spring from causes that are purely organic; causes, which must result in pain and death, however healthful and happy may be the surroundings.

These physical diseases are manifested in infants and young children ; and they have to be subjected to the consequent suffering. No wisdom, tenderness and care of the mother or nurse, after they are born, can wholly avert the painful destiny. The organism is diseased, and the moment the child assumes an independent existence, and begins to be sustained by the action of its own breathing and digestive apparatus, that diseased condition produces its necessary results — pain, and often death.

Two children begin the journey of life, the same hour, and under the same outward surroundings and influences. One is without pain, happy and joyous, and in every expression of its face and motion of its limbs, demonstrates that it feels existence to be bliss and only bliss. The other is distorted with pain, and is wretched. In its every expression and motion, it manifests its sufferings, and its protest against such a painful, wretched existence. The secret of it is this: one is blessed with a healthful, harmonious organization; the other is cursed with a diseased, inharmonious one. We often hear of birthright tendencies to disease — of inherited cancer, scrofula, neuralgia, or consumption. The phrase is most expressive and easily understood. It simply expresses inherited conditions of the physical organism which necessarily result in the particular kind of suffering expressed by these words, when exposed to certain surroundings. Diseased, organic tendencies may be counteracted, and never be allowed to culminate in actual manifestations and suffering, by a wise regulation of outward influences. So of healthful, organic tendencies — these may be, and often are destroyed, by injudicious external treatment.

It is appalling to see the living, sensitive, and most susceptible organism of a child, soon as born, committed to the absolute control of a mother or nurse, who knows and cares nothing about its internal structure, and how to regulate its external treatment and surroundings, in order to its healthful and harmonious development. That tender organism may be formed of tolerably healthy materials, and those materials be harmoniously and happily put together; but the mother knows not how to feed, clothe and handle it. Instead of acquainting herself with human physiology and anatomy, which knowledge is above all price in the mother, and without which no woman is fitted or worthy to be a mother, she spent her girlhood and youth, it may be, in administering to her vanity, her ambition, or in the pursuit of that knowledge and those accomplishments, which can be of little use, except to attract admiration and elicit applause from the worthless. Millions, that are born with tolerably healthy and vigorous bodies, are doomed to a life of suffering and a premature death, by this ignorance of woman in regard to human physiology and anatomy; a knowledge of which can alone fit her to be a mother or a nurse. But, after all, the responsibility of this sad and most baneful and disgraceful ignorance, rests mainly, if not solely, on man. Man never thinks of this as a necessary qualification in the one he chooses for a wife, and the mother of his children, but rather scouts it. Fathers take no thought nor care to have their daughters instructed in this most important of all knowledge, for the mother of the race; their daughters being taught that it is far more important to know how to crochet cats and dogs, and parrots, than to know the interior structure of the human organism, and how to develop it in health and beauty. Brothers feel no interest in the education of their sisters in this science. The church and state have not half the concern in educating the daughters of the land how to treat the human organism in infancy, in order to its vigorous and healthy development, which they show in teaching their sons how to treat and develop, most perfectly, the organic existence of horses and cattle, of pigs and poultry.

It is perfectly truthful to say of this or that bodily disease, —it is often organized into us. Consumption is organized into one, neuralgia into another, cancer into another, scrofula into another, and so on, in regard to every disease with which the human body is organically afflicted. The physical suffering and death resulting from such organic diseases, result from causes so fixed that years will be necessary to counteract them, and restore the organism to soundness. Or, perhaps, restoration is impossible, and that poor, deformed, suffering organism never knew an hour's freedom from pain, from the day of its birth to that of its death.

Amid all the experience and observation that each and every one has, can any one be so bold as to say that our physical destiny is not at all affected by our organic conditions? I think not. About one-third of all that are born in New England die, as to corporeal existence, under five years of age. About two-thirds under fifteen. And this terrible destruction is the result of certain diseased physical conditions and tendencies. · Surely organic conditions do most fatally determine the physical destiny. Even while they live, daily and hourly pain is their bitter portion. Every hour their physical destiny is affected by their organic conditions. In youth, in manhood or womanhood, and even in extreme old age, is physical destiny determined by birthright physical conditions. For how many that die, physically, in these seasons of life attribute their death to inherited diseases? How many suffer thirty, fifty, and seventy years, keenly and terribly, from such diseased tendencies of the physical organism? We must not, cannot, shut our eyes to these facts of life. They meet us at every step. Disease, pain and death are organized into us, and made essential elements of human existence, to a large part of the civilized portions of the race.

CHAPTER V.

PSYCHICAL DESTINY FIXED BY ORGANIZATION.

THE HUMAN SOUL. — What can be said of that? What is it? Of what is it composed! What are the facts in regard to its modes of action, its nature and destiny? It would be easy to deal in fiction; but I would discard fiction, and look at facts. The soul is something that sees and hears, thinks and feels. It is not a thought, but that which thinks; it is not a feeling, but that which feels. I shall assume here, as I have done, that the soul is a substance, a something and not nothing. I shall assume that it is an organized structure, and shall designate it the psychical organism — to distinguish it from the body or physical organism. I shall call its destiny the psychical destiny, as I do that of the body, the physical destiny of man. The question may arise, Of what is the soul composed? We cannot tell. We know not the substances of which it is composed, nor how they are put together. We know it only through its manifestations as these are made known to our consciousness, and to our bodily senses, i. e., to our interior and to our exterior senses. By its fruits we know it, as these are recognized by our interior and exterior experiences. As we know that air, light, electricity and magnetism exist by their fruits, so do we know that the soul exists by its fruits. But we can no more know of what materials the soul is composed by observing its fruits, than we can of what magnetism is composed by seeing its fruits.

Judged by its manifestations, I should conclude the soul to be a compound of material elements, as really as is a bar of iron; differing, of course, in kind; the soul being composed of materials so refined and so potent, that when put together in a certain manner, and placed in certain conditions, it is capable of producing all the phenomena attributed to the soul; that it can see, hear, feel, taste, smell, think, reason, will, love, hate, worship, &c.

The soul is capable of a great variety of manifestations. We classify them, and call one class Reason, another Will, another Love, another Conscience, another Passion, another Hunger, another Thirst, another Hatred, &c. But it is the same soul, acting in various ways, towards different objects, and for different ends. So we group the faculties of the soul, and call one group Intellectual, another Affectional, another Social, another Moral, another Domestic, another Religious. But it is one and the same psychical organism that performs all these operations, making itself manifest towards different objects in different ways, and for different purposes. But, however we may analyze and classify its operations, and reason about its modes and actions, yet we have the same reason to consider it in the light of organized matter, composed of different elements, put together in certain proportions, and that its organic existence is produced by the action of fixed laws, that we have to consider the body in this light.

Does the soul form the body or the body the soul? Does the physical man produce the psychical, or the psychical the physical? It seems most consonant with reason and facts to say that the soul forms the body, the psychical the physical man; that the body, or exterior organism, is an appendage to the soul, or interior organism. The soul, not the body, is the conscious, thinking, feeling, vitalizing power; the real man or woman. The power to attract, absorb, assimilate and construct, is in the soul, not in the body. The soul, not the body, is the motive, plastic power to gather up the materials and construct the body. The body for the soul, not the soul for the body; the physical for the psychical, not the psychical for the physical man.

What the soul *is*, I know not; what it *does*, I know, by consciousness, and by seeing and hearing through my interior and exterior senses. MAN! What is he? A being composed of two distinct organisms, both of which are made up of material substances, one within the other; each essentially dependent on the other for health ·and happiness, while in this state; an outer and inner kingdom; the interior acting through the exterior, and through it manifesting its needs, its thoughts, its emotions, and all its operations, so far as it can be done, but still *capable of an independent existence when the exterior shall have been cast off*. The psychical organism, the inner man, can be seen and heard by the eye and ear of the soul, as the physical organism, or outer man can be seen and heard by the eye and ear of the body. As the physical body can be seen, heard and felt by other physical bodies, so the soul, or psychical body, can be seen, heard and felt, by other souls that have cast off the outer man, and entered upon the life within the veil. As I know what Magnetism does, at least some things that it does, but know not what it is, so I know many things which the soul does, but not what it is. Behold what it does! What are the Governmental, Ecclesiastical, Educational and Commercial Institutions of the world? What are houses, towns, cities, ships, agricultural, manufacturing and mechanical operations and implements? What are all those things that are designed to compel the forces of nature to work for man? Behold every thing that man has invented and done to supply the demands of his body and soul! These all are but outward manifestations of that soul, that gives vitality and power to the body. All that man does, individually and collectively, is but the work of the human soul. What power is in that interior organism! Whatever is found on earth, as the product of human ingenuity, skill, and action, is but the manifestation of this unseen, intangible agent.

Many questions may arise which fancy and curiosity may suggest, and imagination answer. Are souls generated as bodies are? Or, are they created by some direct, arbitrary exertion of power, a soul for each body? At what time in the developmental process does the soul take possession of the body? These and many other questions relating to the human soul, may arise in the mind of the reader, but they are not pertinent to my great object, which is to answer this one question — Is the destiny of the soul or psychical organism determined by its organization? In this respect does the analogy hold good between the soul and body? This I will do what I may to answer.

I have assumed that the soul, like the body, is an organic structure, exactly corresponding with the exterior organism; its vitalizing and motive power permeating and vitalizing every particle of matter in the body — answering to it in form and size, and through it making itself visible, audible and tangible in all its infinitely varied and diversified operations. I have shown that the destiny of the body depends on the kind of materials of which it is composed and on the manner in which they are put together. Do the healthy action and happy destiny of the interior organism depend on the same causes? Is this unseen, intangible, most mysterious organism — this vitalizing, motive, thinking, emotional power, which, in fact, constitutes the man or the woman, like a watch, dependent, for its healthy and happy destiny, on the perfection of its materials, and of its workmanship? If the materials of which a watch is made be ever so perfect, and they be clumsily put together, there will be no harmony of action between the parts, and no confidence will be had in it as an indicator of time. It will be worthless, inasmuch as it cannot answer the end of its existence. Then, again, if the workmanship be ever so perfect, and the materials be unsound and unsuitable for such a purpose as a watch, then its action will be irregular; it will be worthless. It cannot be trusted. Is it thus with the thinking, feeling, rational part of human nature? The psychical organism of man, when made up of right materials, unmixed with alloy, but put together without order or harmony between the several parts; can its destiny be noble and happy? If it ever attains to harmony and happiness, must it not be through much suffering! But suppose the materials to be unsound and unfit, and the putting together be perfect; would not the result be the same? Must not that soul reach the kingdom of heaven through much tribulation? It must. Life, to all such unsound and discordantly formed souls, must spring from death. But when that which thinks, feels, vitalizes, contrives and does all that is designed and done by men, women and children, is composed of sound and fitting materials, and these are harmoniously put together, then the soul comes forth upon the theatre of life, proudly and exultingly takes its place amid the great universe of living beings, with a crown of fadeless beauty and radiant glory before it, and grandly and majestically walks on to take possession. Will any human soul come short of this bright destiny? If so — why? May it not be owing, mainly, to the imperfection of its materials and of the manner of their making up? In a word, to a diseased organization? The history of the human soul is but a series of facts to demonstrate the truth of the position, *that the destiny of each soul is determined by its organization and its constitutional tendencies.*

In this investigation I ignore all discussion of the question of Free Agency and individual responsibility. The consciousness of each man or woman will take care of that. This answers all questions, scatters all doubts, and clears away all darkness in regard to that long and anxiously mooted subject. No matter how strong, nor how multitudinous, nor how learned and astute the arguments may be that are adduced to prove that man, as to character and destiny, is the mere result of chance, or of circumstances; merely the result of a power over which he has no control, and therefore irresponsible for his actions, do what he may; the consciousness of every human being instantly pours contempt upon them all, and makes it certain that, within fixed limits prescribed by the laws of his being, he is free to do, or not to do, and responsible for what he does; that within certain boundaries, prescribed by Nature, the truth and justice of the following requirement are self-evident: OBEY AND LIVE, DISOBEY AND DIE. Self-condemnation and self-inflicted suffering, with the consciousness that they are deserved, will ever accompany our abnormal acts, despite all arguments to prove that we could not help but do them, and that we ought not to suffer for what we were obliged to do.

I have remarked that the Human Race is a Unit, and in all essential characteristics alike, so that any one of that Race may be instantly distinguished from every other species of animated existences. A human being cannot only be distinguished from every other animal, but each one can be recognized as different from each and every other human being. That which marks the difference between human beings, and enables us to distinguish one from another, is no less certain than that which distinguishes man from all other beings. Though all have essentially the same needs and capabilities, yet each one differs from each and every other in his modes of manifestation, or in some way.

INTELLECTUAL POWERS. — We group together certain operations or manifestations of the psychical organism, and designate them as intellectual powers. How deeply these powers are affected by organic conditions, we may not be able to comprehend fully; but the history of the human intellect is but one great fact, going to demonstrate the intimacy of the relation between the intellectual organization and the intellectual destiny of the soul. This lesson is learned most fully from man's intellectual history — that as are the organic conditions of the soul and body, so will be the action of the intellectual faculties both in individuals and communities. As to Direction; Why are the intellectual powers of one directed to one pursuit and of another to another? See the intellect of Zera Colburn directed to mathematical calculations; that of Fulton to the steam-engine; that of Galileo, to Astronomy; that of Newton, to Natural Philosophy; that of Locke and Edwards, to Metaphysics; that of one to Chemistry, of another to Geology, of another to Botany; that of an Audubon, to Ornithology; and that of Franklin, to Electricity. Why was the intellect of Jesus consecrated to the salvation, and that of Napoleon to the destruction of human beings? Why are the intellectual powers of one devoted to Agriculture, of another to Mechanics, and of another to Commerce? See the various objects towards which various minds are directed. Trace the history of Agriculture, or the art of producing the raw materials necessary to feed, clothe, and house man; trace the history of Manufacturing, or the art of preparing those raw materials for use ; trace the history of Commerce, or the art of transporting these necessaries of life from town to town, from city to city, state to state, and from continent to continent. Then trace the history of Governments and Religions, with all their appendages ; the history of Printing, of Books, Newspapers and Writing ; the history of Law, Medicine and Theology, Railways and Electric Telegraphs, the soul using the flashing thunderbolt to herald its thoughts and affections around the world. See what the human intellect has done to create and perfect means to save, to destroy, and to govern human beings, and to feed, clothe, and house them ! Do this, and say, then, if all this variety, this antagonism in results, of the action of man's intellectual powers, can be accounted for except on the principle, that Destiny is determined by Organization ?

It is vain to seek to account for this by educational and adventitious influences, brought to bear on the intellect after birth. The direction of their powers, in many, is manifested before these influences are brought to bear upon them. Witness Zera Colburn, Mozart, Haydn, Napoleon, and above all, the blind slave-child, who has shown such astonishing power of music. Indeed, every infant in the nursery, every child in the school-room and on the play-ground, shows that the human intellect is directed in its pursuits by a power above and behind all post-natal education. The education that gave direction to the intellect of Moses, and of Jesus, of Mohammed, of Krishna, of Luther, of Columbus, of Hume, Knox, Voltaire, and of John Brown, was given in the pre-natal state. So, as to the degree of intellectual activity, as to acuteness, quickness and endurance. How much more acute, intense and enduring the action of the intellectual powers of some minds than others ! No post-natal influences can explain these phenomena ; only that pre-natal influence, which controlled the organization before birth, can explain them; giving to one an organic tendency to one pursuit, and to another, an organic bias to another; and giving to this, the power of intense, concentrated, and enduring activity, and to that, the power only of feeble, shattered, irregular and inefficient action.

How many children are ruined by the efforts of parents to compel them to educate their intellects to pursuits towards which they have no organic or constitutional tendency! By a close observation of facts, all, having the control of children, should seek to acquaint themselves with their organic and constitutional tendencies, and then give them all possible assistance to enable them to pursue those occupations that most coincide with their birthright tendencies. Persons seldom succeed well when they attempt to pursue a calling for which they have no natural bias, and no hearty relish.

As to the Affectional and Sympathetic Powers. — Who can read the history of these powers of the soul and observe their action in all ages, and among all tribes and peoples, and not feel how much our affections and sympathies are controlled by our organic, psychical conditions? How variously directed! One being to one object, and another, to another; this being lovable to one, that to another; the object that seems most lovable and beautiful to one, seeming most unlovable and deformed to another; the woman that is earnestly sought as a wife by one, being as earnestly shunned in that relation by another; the God that seems worthy the supreme love and worship of the Jew, seeming most repulsive to the gentle Nazarene; what, as God, calling out the highest love and devotion of a Mohammedan or Brahmin, but exciting only scorn and contempt in the Christian; the Christ, the Saviour of Christendom, being the cunning impostor and juggler of the Mussulman and Hindoo, and what is lovable and sacred to a Romanist, being contemptible and degrading to the Protestant. What can account for this difference in the direction of our sympathy and love? It is vain to attribute it to a difference in the post-natal influences that bear upon them, for it is more marked in infants and children than in adults. See how these are attracted by some and repelled by others! Watch them in their pairings and matings, in their friendships and enmities! So as to degree, fidelity, depth, intensity and devotion of affection and sympathy. How deep, silent, constant, confiding and long-suffering are they in some; and how shallow, clamorous, obtrusive, fickle, jealous, irritable, impatient and short-lived, in others! How various the modes of manifestation! In one, love and sympathy flowing out in pet names, and terms of endearment, in kisses and personal caresses, as well as in deeds of justice and kindness; and in others, only in practical good works, but never in kisses, caresses and endearing words!

Illustrations of this are found wherever the relations of husband and wife, parent and child, brother and sister, friend and friend exist. And different peoples have distinctive modes of expression. How different the Italian and the Turk, the Frenchman and the German, the Irish and the Scotch, the Spaniard and the African, the Yankee and the Chinese, in the nature and manifestations of their affections and sympathies. No difference of climate, soil, social conditions, food, and education, can account for this diversity. There is a power behind them all, unseen, unheard, but ever felt and ever potent, which determines these varied outward expressions of the love element. These sympathetic and affectional phenomena can be accounted for only on the differences in organic conditions and constitutional tendencies of the soul, created before birth.

3

So of the Passions and Appetites. — Note their actions in individuals and communities, in different tribes and kingdoms. Watch their manifestations among the Indians of the Rocky Mountains, and their neighbors the Mormons; among the Yankees, the Chinese and Russians; in the Slave States and Barbary States; among land pirates and sea pirates; Laplanders and the Bedouin Arabs. Each tribe, state, nation and people, have their peculiar ways of manifesting anger, envy, jealousy, revenge, ambition and avarice. How various the manifestations among children! Some are born with an organic tendency to tea, coffee, tobacco, alcohol, opium, and other narcotic and alcoholic stimulants, and some with a deep-seated aversion to these. Some have a constitutional tendency to steal and rob, to murder and piracy. Man-stealing or kidnapping, is a prominent characteristic of the Slave States; man-killing, of the people of England, France, and of all nations, and armies of disciplined man-killers are organized and maintained to gratify this propensity. Ask for the cause, and it will be found in the organic conditions of the souls of the different people. Theft being organized into the soul of one, murder and piracy into that of another; the spirit and idea of freedom into one, slave-hunting and slave-driving into another. Drunkenness, war, negro-hatred into one, total abstinence, peace, and respect for human rights, into others. So of Presbyterianism, Methodism, Unitarianism, Universalism, Calvinism, Mohammedanism and Hindooism, and sectarisms of all kinds are organized into the soul before birth, and become its organic conditions. Religious views and customs are organized into the souls of all people, more or less. A revengeful, sensual, cautious, coarse organization, will have corresponding conceptions of God. Each must see God in the mirror of his own soul. If that mirror be pure, bright, and polished, the soul will have a clear, bright conception of God; but if our mirror be obscure, we shall have an obscure conception of God. So our worship will correspond to our organization. The healthfully organized soul, alone, can worship God in spirit and in truth. Those whose souls glow with love and good will to man, will see and worship God in men, women and children; those who have little regard for man, will see and worship God in times and places, and in rites and ceremonies. Religion refers especially to the relations between man and man. As are our organic psychical conditions, so will be our conceptions of man and his relations to man. The gross, sensual, psychical organism, will regard the distinction of sex as a mere means of sensual indulgence, and marriage simply as a license to render it legal and respectable. He will see woman through the medium of his own animalism. What shall be said of tendencies to idiocy and insanity? Do these result from defects in the organization of the soul, or of the body? In malformations of the body which render it impossible for the soul to manifest itself truly and healthfully through it, or in permanent defects in the psychical organism? This question will one day receive an answer. I cannot give it, nor can any one in the present imperfect knowledge of the relations between the body and soul. But as to the lying, deceit, dishonesty, injustice, licentiousness, theft, robbery, murder and tyranny of mankind, these may hereafter be found to result more from defects in the organic conditions of the soul, than in outward surroundings.

The following is from Draper's "Human Physiology": "During the process of the development of the intellect of man, various psychical persuasions in succession arise, which are frequently imputed to education or tradition, but of which the origin is undoubtedly to be traced to the organization. Those general ideas that are found all over the world, among

all races of mankind, whatever may be the climate in which
they live, their social condition or religious opinions, — ideas
of what is good and evil, of virtue, of the efficacy of penance
and of prayer, of rewards and punishments, and of another
world; these, from the uniformity of their existence in all
ages, and in all places, must be imputed to the stamp that
has been put upon our cerebral organization. Universal
opinions are not the result of accident, nor always of tradition. They are often creations of the mind, arising from
peculiarities of constitution."

This, then, is Man; a being composed of two organic
structures — one within the other — giving to it life and motion. A kingdom within a kingdom — the treasures of which
are, as yet, but little known. The Interior constructs and
controls the Exterior kingdom, under the direction of that
God who controls all things. The body exists for the soul,
not the soul for the body. The soul is the permanent, ever-
living, ever-progressing organism, the immortal Man or
Woman; the body is but an incident to the soul, as a garment is to the body. THE BODY FOR THE SOUL, NOT THE
SOUL FOR THE BODY! Therefore, never sacrifice the soul
to the body. Never dishonor nor degrade the soul to supply
the demands of the body, or even to preserve it from outrage
and death. Keep the soul pure and sacred, whatever becomes
of the body. In an harmoniously organized body and soul
there can be no conflict. The demands of each will correspond with the demands of the other.

These two organisms — the physical and psychical, or the
body and soul — are ever acting and reacting each upon the
other. Every action of the body, every pulsation of the
heart, every effort of the brain, lungs, stomach, and the various
vital functions of the body, affect the condition of the soul. It
is very hard for the soul to keep in a serene and happy state

while the body is tortured with nervous headache, or jumping toothache, or agonizing dyspepsia. So the soul affects the body. When the psychical organism is exercised with grief, sorrow, anger, revenge, despondence, or any intellectual or affectional derangement, the physical organism is always more or less affected thereby. The health and life of the body must necessarily be deeply affected by those physical conditions and tendencies that were organized into it before birth. So the health and life of the soul must be deeply affected by the pre-natal tendencies that were organized into it. So the destiny of each organism must be deeply affected by the organic conditions of the other.

The power that controls the organization must, to a great extent, if not entirely, control the character and destiny of the man or woman ; inasmuch as human life, in all relations, results from organic conditions and constitutional tendencies, more than from any or all outward surroundings. Where is that power that controls the organic conditions and birthright tendencies of human beings? If we can find this, we find the power that moulds the character and shapes the destiny of individuals and nations.

CHAPTER VI.

ORGANIZATION DETERMINED BY MATERNAL CONDITIONS.

In the two preceding chapters I have shown, that, DESTINY
IS DETERMINED BY ORGANIZATION. Whatever influence,
material, domestic, social, political, ecclesiastical, commercial
and literary surroundings may have on human character
and destiny, it is mainly exerted indirectly. *Home Influences*
do more to give tone and direction to our feelings, thoughts
and aspirations, and to our outward actions, and to shape our
hourly, daily, and eternal destiny, than all other external
influences combined. But what controls men and women in
the selection of life-companions that are to decide what those
home-influences shall be? For the influence of home, for
good or evil, depends, solely, on the relations that exist
between the husband and wife. If love is the bond, the
influence will be good; if anything else, it will be evil and
only evil. In no relation is the truth of the maxim, that
destiny is determined by organization, so clearly made manifest, as in that of husband and wife. In entering into the
conjugal relation, in their loyalty to it, and in their treatment
of each other in it, the phenomena of life can be accounted
for, only, by regarding them as the results of the organic
conditions of the actors in the strange, inexplicable drama.
No adventitious, outward causes, can account for these often

unexpected and sad results. These home-influences, instead of directly controlling the organization of the husband and wife, are controlled by it. So that the character of any domestic circle may be known by the character of the organizations of the individuals that compose it, especially by that of the husband and wife; for, as is their organization, so is that of their children. What controls men and women in seeking wives or husbands? Organic conditions — mainly.

So of Social Relations, Outside of Home. External influences do, indeed, affect us deeply in our daily and hourly life and destiny, but, only, indirectly. But what controls us in the selection of friends and associates? What guides us in our treatment of, and manifestations to one another, in social gatherings, and in our social intercourse generally? Our organization, unquestionably, to a great extent; and the character of our associates is, generally, a pretty sure test of our organic conditions, and our birthright, constitutional tendencies. Thus, instead of our organic conditions being controlled by our social surroundings, these, and the destiny they bring to us, are determined by them. As is our organization, so will be our social relations and destiny.

So of our Religion. True, our destiny is affected by our theological opinions and ecclesiastical relations; but it is no less true that these opinions and relations are determined, mainly, by our organizations. No matter to what sect of religionists we belong, it will be found that we have a constitutional, pre-natal tendency to the opinions and practices of that sect. The Calvinist will be found to have an organic bias towards a stern God of vengeance; a Methodist, towards loud, vociferous, outward demonstrations; a Quaker, towards a quiet, contemplative mode of worship. So throughout all religions; as is our organization, so will be our religious opinions and customs.

So of our Occupations, our Amusements, and our Political Relations. As a general rule, as is our organization, so will be our occupations, our amusements, and our political opinions and practices. Instead of being directly determined by these, our organic conditions determine what they shall be. The domestic, social, political, religious, literary and commercial relations and institutions of Massachusetts and South Carolina, constitute an index to the organic conditions and constitutional tendencies of their respective peoples; the bias of the people of the former is to knowledge, justice, freedom and civilization; that of the people of the latter is to ignorance, injustice, slavery, theft, robbery and barbarism. The people of Massachusetts are prone to live by honest and honorable labor; South Carolina is prone to live by theft and robbery, and by making merchandise of her own sons and daughters.

So of Climate, Soil, and all Material Surroundings. These do not directly give character to the organic conditions of the people, but our organization gives character to them; i. e., these affect us according to our organization. As are our organic conditions, so will be the impressions made on us by our material surroundings. The soul, or psychical organism, is the mirror presented to us by the mother, to enable us to behold the exterior world; and, by a fixed law of our being, our conceptions of external objects depend on the condition of that mirror. It is in that psychical mirror that we behold all objects outside of ourselves. Our conceptions of God, and of eternal life; our conceptions of man, and his relations to God and immortality, and to his fellow-beings; our conceptions of the distinction of sex, of its nature and its object, and of the relations between men and women, and of the mission of woman to man, and of man to woman; in a word, all our conceptions of ourselves, in our relations to the material, intellectual, social, and spiritual universe, so full of the vast, the beautiful, the sublime, the mysterious and incomprehensible, are mainly characterized by those organic conditions and constitutional tendencies that our mothers gave to us in our pre-natal life. A healthful, harmonious psychical organization, or soul-mirror, will reflect external objects to us as they are ; but to a diseased, discordant organization, all must seem distorted.

Thus, organization determines the character and destiny ; but who or what determines the organization? The power which controls that, controls its results. Man makes the state ; who makes the man? Man organizes and administers the ecclesiastical, governmental, literary and commercial institutions of the world ; who organizes and administers the man? Man gathers up materials and builds houses, palaces, temples, ships, towns and cities ; but who gathers together the materials and builds up the man? Man, having selected fitting materials, constructs railroads, locomotives, steamengines, watches, clocks, thermometers, barometers, compasses, telegraphs and chemical apparatus, and all the machinery designed to prepare the raw material for food and raiment ; but who gathers together the fitting materials and forms them into that most delicate, most mysterious, wonderful and potential of all structures — a living, rational, aspiring, immortal man? But one answer can be given to these questions ; i. e., THE MOTHER ! So far as human agency is concerned, THE MOTHER MAKES THE MAN ; the father's influence being exerted, after conception, indirectly through the mother. My object being to consider the Empire of the Mother, I shall not now discuss the influence of the father.

" God gave to man dominion over the beasts of the field, the fowls of the air, and the fish of the sea," but to whom did God give dominion over man? Not to kings and queens,

3 *

nor to presidents and potentates; not to parliaments and congresses, nor to priests and politicians; not to church and state, nor to armies and navies; not to the pulpit and the press, nor to the school and the college — but to the mother. These all have their place as means of controlling human character, and shaping human destiny; but to the mother hath God said, " thy kingdom is an everlasting kingdom, and thy dominion is without end." The God of Nature never committed the destiny of man, as individuals, as families, as societies, as states and nations, to a soulless corporation called a church or government; but, as to the exercise of direction and control over the interior and exterior life of man, God says to the mother, " under me, thine is the kingdom, and the power, and the glory." The mother, not the pope nor the king, not the church nor the state, is God's vicegerent, to determine the place of each upon the scroll of destiny.

But how does the mother thus hold the sceptre of dominion over individuals and states? What are the agencies by which her power is exercised? She rules the world, not by brute force; for armies and navies, with their array of means to mutilate and kill human bodies, constitute no part of her power. Military force, in her kingdom, is utterly ignored as an element of strength. Nor does she rule by arbitrary, external authority; nor yet by capricious, arbitrary legislation. The machinery of violence, by which human bodies are ruled by man, is unknown to her sovereignty over the race. The same may be said of the ballot; she rules no more by ballots than by bullets. She does indeed rule the great human family, in and out of the body, by laws; but these laws are not enacted by Congress nor Parliament; nor are they engraven on parchment; nor are they executed by constables and sheriffs; but, through the powers and functions of her body and soul, they are enacted by the All-wise, the All-just, and All-powerful; and, through her means, are engraven on the body and soul of each one, as essential conditions of life and health; and they are self-executing. As a birthright inheritance, the Mother presents to each child a code of just and perfect laws, which, if unobstructed, would work out for it a sublime and happy destiny. Blessed is that child whose birthright code is not dishonored and defaced by the presence of unconstitutional, unnatural, pernicious, temporary by-laws.

The august drama of human life; the secret, unseen causes and history of human character and destiny, may be written in two short sentences, i. e.: DESTINY IS DETERMINED BY ORGANIZATION — ORGANIZATION IS DETERMINED BY MATERNAL CONDITIONS. The story of the internal and external experiences of individuals, and of states and nations, is told in these two expressions. The destiny of man, whether acting as an individual, or as a church, nation, or empire, is wrapt up in his organization; the character of that organization is hidden away in the silent depths of the mother's organism. Every human being is a living fact to demonstrate this. Those who are accustomed to trace the phenomena of human life, as manifested in individuals and combination, to their antecedents, will find no lack of facts to illustrate this. Take the following.

Organic tendency to Useful Labor. D. P. is a woman whose experience is instructive. She lives but to labor; not for love of gain, but from the love of useful action. She never wastes her energies in labors that benefit no one; but they are ever directed to something useful. A restless, anxious spirit, which she cannot control, is ever prompting her to useful and benevolent action, in household labors, in out-door exercise, and in actions that are beneficial to her neighbors. From childhood, the same uncontrollable desire to be useful to somebody, has led her onward and governed her actions. *The Cause.* From her conception to her birth, one irrepressible desire governed the activities of her mother. All her energies of soul and body were directed to useful ends. She was ever on the alert to find opportunities to do good to somebody. She literally went about doing good, and ever found it "more blessed to give than receive." The same tendencies appeared in her child at a very early age. Even as a child, she was ever devising some plans that had in view the good of others, and had an extraordinary aptitude to execute her own benevolent purposes. Hers was a rich and glorious inheritance. Would that a similar organization could be the birthright legacy of every child from its mother. How soon would human beings cease to inflict injuries on others for their own benefit.

The Child Visitor. Another fact to illustrate the power of the mother over the organic conditions of her child. · L. F., ten years old, never can rest at home. She is ever running here and there, restless as a wild bird in a cage, just from the woods. She ever pines to be abroad. Is ever teasing her mother to let her go visiting. Knows no rest, no enjoyment, except in going from house to house, making calls, and getting up parties among her mates. Visiting seems to be the one overmastering thought and passion of her life. *Cause.* The father was a hard man, a drinking man, and the terror of his wife. During her child's entire pre-natal life, to avoid him the mother was abroad, making calls, going from house to house, getting up parties and making visits. Her entire waking hours, during that period, were thus spent. She saved her child from the drunken father's influence; but she stamped upon it the stamp of a restless visitor, and unfitted her for any steady, useful employment. It will prove a sad legacy to the child, as she passes on to womanhood, and enters into the natural relations and encounters the stern realities of life, as a wife, a mother, and actor in the great drama of humanity.

In every family and neighborhood are to be found facts that strikingly illustrate the truth of the position, that, organization is determined by maternal conditions; that the conditions of the maternal organism do, and must, of necessity, to a great extent, determine the character of that organization which is developed within it. Indeed, each and every man or woman is but a fact which serves to illustrate and confirm this truth.

Maternal Associations. Some thirty years ago it was my privilege to take an active part in the formation of many Maternal Associations — the object of which was to receive and give light in regard to the function, the responsibilities and duties of maternity. Only mothers composed the associations. For two years I met with these associations, averaging over once a week, and recorded in my private journal the subjects that were discussed in them, the average attendance being about twenty mothers. The mothers used to give accounts of the peculiar characteristics of their children; of their dispositions and tempers; their aptitudes and inclinations in regard to food, drink, dress, amusements, and occupations; of their peculiar tendencies to this or that occupation or amusement. The transmission of physical and psychical conditions and qualities from mothers to their children; the pre-natal education and gestational life and history of their children were freely discussed, and the bearing of the impressions made on children before birth, on their character and happiness afterwards; the bearings of maternal conditions during the pre-natal life of children on their organization, and on the character and destiny that should result from it; the pre-natal rights of children to a love origin, and

to healthy bodies and healthy souls, and to a welcome into
life from both parents and from the entire community; to
what extent the character and destiny of a child can be
known from a knowledge of the diseases that lurk in the
mother's blood, and of the intellectual, social and spiritual
conditions of her soul; the relation between the mother's
food, drink, labor and amusements and the conditions of her
blood, and between her blood and the organic existence, and
the character and destiny of her child; these and like subjects were freely and anxiously discussed in those meetings
of mothers. The plan of keeping a written record of their
physical and psychical conditions and experiences during the
pre-natal development of their children, was suggested to those
mothers; that they might be able to see to what extent the
post-natal character and destiny of those children corresponded
with the conditions and experiences of their mothers during
their pre-natal life. Many of those mothers adopted that plan;
and the results were astounding to themselves. Not one of
those mothers but was thoroughly convinced that Organization
was determined by maternal conditions. Some of those jour-
nals were put into my hands to be read, and that I might take
from them such extracts as I could make useful in discussing,
publicly, the pre-natal rights of children, the responsibility of
mothers, and their empire over the character and destiny of
the race. I learned more concerning the hidden sources
of the peculiarities and manifestations in the individual, domestic, social, political and religious life of man, from those
mothers, than I had ever learned before from books, schools
and colleges. If intelligent, loving and observing mothers
would keep records of their physical and psychical conditions
during the pre-natal life and education of their children, it
would be of more value to the world, and do more to give a
true insight into the nature, character and destiny of man,

than histories of states and nations. The value of maternal associations for a free and full interchange of thought and feeling, touching the power of the mother over the organization of her child, and through that, over its character and destiny after its birth, can never be overestimated. When the Age of Fiction, in regard to man, his character, his relations and destiny, shall have given place to the Age of Fact, and these shall be regarded as the results of antecedents that may be controlled, to a great extent, by human agency, then will the empire of woman, as a mother, be known and appreciated. It will be seen that her organism is the hiding-place of that power which watches over and controls the destiny of individuals and of nations ; and that, through the mother, not through the church, nor the state, the kingdom of God is to be incarnated in human life, and his " will be done on earth as it is in heaven." If the prayer, " *Thy kingdom come,*" is ever to be answered on earth, it must be answered, not by the church, nor the state, but by the mother. To the mother, under God, must be ascribed the glory of that event, if it ever occurs.

CHAPTER VII.

ORGANIC EXISTENCE — WHERE FORMED?

THE question arises — Has the mother any power over the quality of the materials of which the organism of her child, body and soul, shall be formed, and as to the manner in which these materials shall be put together? The question is direct, plain, and easy to be understood; but put in words such as we use in regard to any structure, organic or inorganic, whether the result of human or divine agency. Whether we look at an elephant or a fly, a man or a muscle, a ship or a clock, three questions naturally arise — *Who* made it? Of *what* is it made? *How* is it made? So in regard to the human organism, or person; in examining it, we naturally ask — *Who* made it? Of *what* is it made? *How* is it made? I am considering human beings as to their existence, character and destiny, solely from the stand-point of human agency; more especially of the agency of the mother.

I have said that the parents of each child are responsible for its existence, inasmuch as it is the result of their united and voluntary agency. The mother is as really responsible for her child's existence as is the gardener for the existence of a rose, as the mechanic for the existence of a house, as the farmer for the existence of a field of wheat, which had never existed but for their agency. Arsenic is an enemy to animal life. I make it, take it, and die. Who kills me? Food is a law of life. I refuse to take it, and die. Who kills me? No one doubts my responsibility here. My death is the result of my own agency.

So the act of the mother is the antecedent of the child's existence. Every mother should feel that the whole responsibility rests on her, as really as if no other being had to do with it; for so it does. I do not say she is *alone* in the responsibility, for she is not; the same amount of responsibility rests with the father. He does not *share* it with her. There can be no division, no sharing of responsibility in the Chancery of Heaven. A million vote for slavery, or for war. Each of them is responsible before God for all the wrongs and outrages that belong to those evils, and without which they cannot exist. If the slaveholder is a thief, a robber, a kidnapper, a ruffian and a land-pirate, the man who votes for slavery is the same, and ought to be and will be, ere long, so regarded and treated. So the responsibility of the child's existence rests wholly and undividedly with each parent. The mother is as responsible as if it resulted from her agency alone ; so is the father ; for the exertion of their power to give existence to a child was a matter of choice and not of necessity. The responsibility of each is independent of the other.

But the question — Of what materials is that organism made? and how are they put together? would lead to a description of its chemical analysis and of the laws of combination, which, though of deep interest, is not pertinent to my object. But the question regarding the mother's power over the *kind* of materials of which it shall be composed, and the *manner* of their combination, exactly accords with the end at which I aim. In answering this query I must recur to some facts relating to our organic existence and conditions. One of these facts is suggested by the inquiry — *where* is the Human Organism made up? To this query but one answer can be given, i. e.,

Fact First. — THE ORGANIC EXISTENCE OF EVERY CHILD IS BEGUN AND COMPLETED WITHIN THE ORGANISM OF THE MOTHER.

The question is not, where was the first human organism, or the first man and woman developed or constructed? However interesting this might be, as a matter of speculation, we have no facts to guide us in such an investigation. As well ask — Where was God developed? so far as facts are concerned. It may be that in the future progress of mind in knowledge, facts will be brought to light to justify us in some fixed and certain conclusions in regard to the place where the first human germs were developed. I think we may, from ascertained facts, assume the truth of the following conclusions : —

That the germ existed before the human organism existed. As the acorn existed before the oak, so the germ existed before the man.

That the distinction of sex is in the germ ; that in the process of development, wherever that may have been effected, the masculine germ assumed an organism, adapted to express its peculiar nature and to respond to its peculiar demands ; and the feminine germ, an organism, suited to its nature and necessities. So that, by a fixed law of sexuality, wherever the one assumes a living, visible, tangible form, the other must accompany it as a necessity of its being, in order to meet an ever-present demand of its existence, and to its perfection and happiness ; to its complete salvation.

That the human organism — body and soul — is formed of elements, or substances, that are inherent in and derived from this planet. Whatever these elements may be, and whatever manifestations they may make after they are constructed into human forms, they are all derived from this planet; so that man is, in truth, of the earth. No matter what names are given to that organism and to different parts; call one part body, and another soul; one part flesh, and another spirit; one part matter, another mind; one mortal, the other immortal; one human, the other divine; it is all the same: all men and women, in their entire nature, are made up of elements derived from this planet. So of every mineral, vegetable, and animal production on the earth; the substances of which they are made, are derived from the planet on which they exist. So in regard to all the planets that traverse space; whatever forms exist in Saturn, Jupiter, Mercury, or any other planet, derive the materials of which they are composed, from that planet on which they have their being.

Waiving all further remarks on these topics, we know the fact, that the organic existence of every human being is begun and completed within the organism of the mother. From the moment in which she takes charge of the germ of a new life, and it is located in its natural and appropriate place for development, a process is commenced, which, if undisturbed, must result, by a fixed law of generation, in the formation of a human body and soul. Elements or materials are collected and gathered around that germ, and so arranged and blended with it as to develop from it bones, muscles, nerves, brains, heart, lungs, stomach, liver, eyes, ears, and every organ essential to make a human body; and also a soul, or life-principle, or vital and motive power, with all its powers to think, reason, will, love, and to present all the phenomena and manifestations that demonstrate the presence of a human soul. All these essential ingredients and attributes of the human organism are developed from that germ by a process of selection, accumulation, assimilation, distribution and organization. In the brief space of nine months, that which was scarcely visible to the naked eye, and which, when seen through a microscope, seemed but an oblong or square cell, called the germ-cell, assumes the form of a human being, with all the organs and attributes of a man or a woman.

This most mysterious, inexplicable and wonderful process of developing that minute cell into a human body and soul, is begun and completed within the consecrated precincts of the maternal organism, and beneath the pulsation of the maternal heart. Consider the nature, the character, the power and destiny of the being that is to result from the process that is going on within that sacred enclosure! See the part which it must act in the great drama of life; the theatre on which it is to act, and the countless millions that are to be its companions; consider its pathway into the unending future, the obstacles that lie in its way, and the stern and terrible conflicts it must encounter. Who can contemplate the results of that developmental process, without an overwhelming sense of the grand and the august, as well as of the most endearing affection and tenderness! All that is pure, holy, loving, gentle, and God-like in our nature is called into action, as we trace the history of a life-germ of humanity in its process of development into a living human organism, within the organism of woman. All that have been born of woman in the dead Past, all who constitute the living Present, and all who are to exist on this planet in the hidden Future, have passed, or must hereafter pass, through this unfolding process within her organism; the Holy of Holies of that great temple of humanity which is to enlarge its dimensions, and grow more symmetrical and beautiful in the cycles of Eternity. From woman's organism must come those organic conditions and inborn tendencies that are to shape the character and control the destiny of the future of the human race.

MAN! Behold the organism of woman! Look upon it tenderly and reverently, for within it God has hidden the scroll of destiny to individuals, families, states and nations. There God has laid away the book of his laws for the government of the race. Oh man! spare the person of woman. Harm it not. But ever anxiously labor to develop it in all its functions, into healthful and vigorous activity, and into the perfection of grace and beauty.

HUSBAND! Behold the organism of your wife. Treat it tenderly and reverently. Proudly and graciously bow your manly soul before it in heartfelt and earnest worship; for within that form, so fondly cherished, and so protectingly held to your heart, God has hidden your life as a husband and a father. As a husband, would you have your heart cheered, your life made joyous, and your home your heaven, by the sustaining sympathy, the joyous presence, and all-trusting love of a healthy, happy wife? As a father, would you have around you the glad hearts, the bright faces, and merry voices of healthy children? Then most tenderly and reverently cherish and protect from all harm, the person of your wife; for within that sacred temple, so beautiful and consecrated to you, are concealed the purity, the peace, the dignity, the glory, the very angel guardian of your home.

FATHER! Tenderly and reverently guard and cherish the organism of your daughter. In infancy, childhood and youth, anxiously and constantly protect it from harm, as you would your own soul; for within that organism is written the history, not only of individual men and women, but of the homes, the states and kingdoms of the Future. Be tender of that form, so beautiful and sacred to you, for from it are to issue life or death, joy or sorrow, to the people of the future.

BROTHER! Tenderly and reverently cherish the organism of your sister, and guard it from all harm. Let no injury, no disease, no suffering come to it which you can ward off. Consecrate your youthful zeal, your brotherly sympathy, affection and energy, to shield that loved and beautiful sisterly form from all harm, for in it may be enshrined the destiny of unborn millions.

What are banks, railways, currency and commerce, in their relations to the power, the stability, prosperity and perpetuity of states and kingdoms, compared to the organism of woman? The organic existence of all their subjects with all the conditions and tendencies, the beauty, health and vigor that pertain to it, must be begun and completed in that organism.

Why should not governments look after the health, the beauty, the perfection, and the power of that source from which all their citizens are to derive their existence, their health, energy and powers of endurance, and the state its prosperity, its protection, and glory? They should. The health of the Maternal Organism will be a prominent, perhaps the most prominent object of consideration to a government that consults the physical, intellectual, social and spiritual elevation and happiness of its subjects, and that wisely seeks to save its citizens from the miseries of drunkenness, war and slavery; to avert from them disease, and give them health, and to insure to them life, liberty and happiness. When legislators and statesmen shall see and appreciate the relation of the maternal organism to the peace, prosperity, stability and glory of states and nations, then will governments make the health of woman the object of their most anxious solicitude.

Is it a wonder that the human soul should cling so tenaciously, so tenderly and so trustingly to the mother, within whose sacred and consecrated organism the organic existence of all are perfected? Within which, whatever is beautiful, symmetrical, delicate, complicated and vigorous in our bodies, and whatever is rational, intuitional, clairvoyant, loving, thinking, living and immortal in our souls, was organized into us and made essential attributes of corporeal and incorporeal, of present and eternal life? Is it strange that the purest, most sacred and endearing affections of the human heart should twine around the maternal organism? Whether in the bright looks and elastic movements of the young mother, or in the matronly dignity of middle life, or the decay and decrepitude of age, that sacred form is encircled with hallowed beauty, and radiant with glory. Man may set at nought the restraints of church and state, but the power of the mother can never be wholly and permanently cast off. This, like the power of God, holds him in a grasp which never can be broken.

In this planet exist all the materials that are necessary to the formation of a living human organism, with all its capabilities and its distinctive attributes. These materials must be gathered up, prepared, put together, assimilated, organized and vitalized, and made into living men and women. This work, so full of love and tenderness, so delicate, so complicated, so august, so replete with the destiny of individuals, and of states and kingdoms, and before which the formation and administration of governments sink into insignificance, must be begun and completed not only within the maternal organism, but under the direction and control of that plastic power by which it is vitalized. Of all its attributes or powers, this plasticity of the maternal organism, this power to gather up, to combine, to assimilate, and organize the elements of this planet into human forms, and to vitalize those forms, and make them living and immortal souls, is the most mysterious and sublime. Man is not invested with that power; it is the sole and distinctive attribute of woman. Man may gather up the materials of the earth that are scattered here and there, and build ships and houses, locomotives, railroads, clocks, watches, cities and palaces; states and nations may gather up materials and construct and manage armies and navies, with all the apparatus of war; but men, whether acting as individuals or states and kingdoms, can never gather up, combine and organize the materials of this planet into the bodies and souls of men and women. This power, the most energizing and living with which God has endowed human beings, is woman's sole and exclusive prerogative; and it invests her with majesty and glory, second only to that which surrounds the Almighty. The power of Victoria as a Queen, is contemptible and evanescent compared to the power of Victoria as a Mother. As a Queen, all she does is comparatively trifling in value and evanescent in duration; but, as a Mother, she gathers up the forces and materials, innate in the planet, and fashions them into living organisms but little lower than angels, crowns them with glory and honor, and stamps on them the image of God, and the impress of eternity.

This power, I have said, is woman's exclusive prerogative. The father has no direct control over the organization of the child after conception. The process of organization does not commence till the mother takes charge of the germ, and it is placed within reach of its proper nutriment. Therefore, the father can influence the organic existence of the child, only, by his power over the germ, before the mother takes charge of it, and by influencing it, through her thoughts and feelings, after conception. Before the mother takes charge of the germ, the father may stamp upon it his own peculiarities, whether for health or disease, whether for happiness or misery ; and these peculiarities may become prominent characteristics of the child after it is born ; but after conception, the father can have no control over the organization of the child, except through his power over the affections and sympathies of the mother.   The father may deeply affect the character and destiny of the child ; but his conditions cannot be organized into it as are the conditions of the mother; because its organic existence is not begun and completed in his organism, but in hers.   The mother's power over the constitutional and organic tendencies and predispositions of the child must of necessity be all but absolute ; inasmuch as under the action of the forces of her organism, the entire process of organization is performed.

Much might be, ought to be, and will be said about the power of the father over the character and destiny of his child, and of the manner in which that power is brought to bear on its organization, both before its conception, and between its conception and birth.   Especially will the treatment of the mother by the father of her child during its gestational development, and when all the energies of her body and soul should be left perfectly free from all other sources of exhaustion, to concentrate themselves on the just and rightful performance of the mighty and momentous work in which she is engaged — that of giving a healthy and perfect organization to her child — become a subject of most anxious thought and inquiry to every father, to every friend of progress, and to every church and state, whose aim is the elevation and happiness of man.   But my subject is the empire of the mother.

4

CHAPTER VIII.

THE HUMAN ORGANISM — WHENCE ITS MATERIALS?

WHAT power has the mother over the quality of the materials of which her child is composed, and over the manner in which they are put together? Has she any? If any, what? I refer to the periods of gestation and lactation. As proof that she has power over the *matter* and *manner* of its organization, I have adduced the fact, that the organic existence of every child is begun and completed within the organism of the mother. To this end, I would present another fact, i. e. :

Fact Second. — THE ELEMENTS OF WHICH THE CHILD IS FORMED COME DIRECTLY FROM THE MOTHER'S BLOOD.

To the question—Whence the materials of which the child, previous to birth, is composed? but one answer can be given — *the mother's blood.* From whatever source they may be derived, originally, whether from Earth, Herschel, Saturn, or some other planet, we know that the maternal blood is the only direct channel through which all must come, which is necessary to make up the child's living organism, previous to birth. From the moment in which the developmental process begins, no other source is open to furnish materials for its growth. It may be asked — Whence the materials to form the maternal blood? No matter how this may be answered ; whether that be composed of elements derived from light, heat, air, water, earth, vegetable or animal food, or from all combined, from this or from some other planet, — the fact is before us, clear and unmistakable, that the blood of the mother is the only source of all direct nutrition during the pre-natal life of the child; till it assumes the form of a human being complete in all its parts, and prepared for an existence independent of the mother.

That this is true of the visible, or flesh and blood organism, no one will dispute. By a process of chemical analysis, it is demonstrated to the physical senses that all the elements that compose the human body are found in the blood of woman ; and the means, by which they are conveyed to the growing child, can be made manifest. So it can be known, as any fact, made evident to the senses, can be known, that all which goes to make up each and every part of the human body, before birth, comes directly from this source. A perfect physical organism must have bones, muscles, sinews, nerves, heart, brain, stomach, lungs, eyes, ears, &c. ; and all these, though so different in their structure, use, and appearance, must all be derived from one and the same source. Therefore, all the elements necessary when properly selected and put together, to make these different organs and parts of a human organism, must exist in the blood of woman.

So far as the body is concerned, all this can be made certain by a demonstration which, like figures, cannot lie. The eye, the brain, the heart, the stomach, and every other part of the system can be analyzed, the component parts of each separated and subjected to the inspection of the senses ; and each separate part of these organs, and of the whole body, be found in the maternal blood. So that no doubt can exist, that all the materials that go to make up the *physical* organism before birth, must come directly from this source.

But the soul, or *psychical* organism: Is this a substance? Is it an organized structure? If so (and I assume that it is), whence the materials of which it is composed? This is formed of different and more subtle and refined materials than the physical, which, when combined in a certain form and manner, make a human soul, mind, or spirit (no matter · as to its name), which is capable of all the phenomena of thought, feeling, will, reason, and all others which are manifestations of what we call soul. Whether this be a compound of organized substances, or whether it be made up of one element, or what may be its shape, or what the changes to which it is liable; these are questions not important to the object at which I aim; though my conviction is that the portion of the living human organism which thinks, reasons, feels, loves, contrives, aspires; which sees, hears, tastes and smells; and which vitalizes every particle and portion of the body, and is the motive power of the whole system,—is an organized substance, or rather a compound of organized substances, having the exact form and appearance of a man or woman, and that this psychical organism is the exact counterpart of the physical; or rather, the latter is the exact counterpart of the former; the physical exactly answering to the psychical in every particular, being made by it, and for it; and in every particle of its structure being permeated and vitalized by it, and its existence having no significance, except as a medium formed by the spirit, or psychical organism, and adapted to the manifestation of all its peculiar qualities.

Assuming, then, that the soul, or the thinking, feeling, willing, vitalizing and motive power of the human organism is an organized substance, or, a compound of organized substances; that it is something and not nothing; the same question arises in regard to it that is asked in reference to the body — Whence the elements or materials of which it is formed? They must come from some source, and that source must be within reach of and accessible to the plastic or forming power, whatever, or wherever that power may be. If there be any soul or living power in the germ capable of conscious thought, affection, memory, will and reason, it lies beyond our ken. Whatever other power may be there, this is not, so far as we can discover, any more than there is a body, with brains, eyes, heart and lungs and stomach. There is a something in the germ, which, under the fostering care, and aided by the vitalizing, constructive power of the maternal organism, is competent to gather up materials from its surroundings, and so distribute, assimilate, combine and unite them, as to present them, in due time, in the form of a living, self-moving human being. This power to gather up those materials and form them into a living child, is in the germ ; but it could never perform this work only within the living organism of woman ; and in direct contact with her blood, and aided by the plastic power of her nature. If there is, or ever was, any other place or organism, in which a human germ could be developed into a human being, except the organism of woman, thus far, human research has failed to discover it.

The psychical organism must derive its materials from the same source from which the body is derived. Woman's blood is the immediate source from which come all human souls as well as bodies. This psychical organism, or soul, constitutes the vitalizing, thinking, loving and motive power of the flesh and blood organism, its life-principle. The physical body has material eyes and ears, but it is the psychical organism that sees and hears ; the physical has nerves, but it is the psychical that feels, smells and tastes ; the body has legs, but it is the soul that walks ; and the body has a tongue, but it is the soul that talks. So of all the organs and functions of the physical organism ; they would all be as wood and stone cut and carved into the likeness of a man or woman, utterly destitute of life and motion, and of thought and feeling, of will and memory, but for the thinking, feeling, living, willing psychical organism within. This vitalizes every organ and function of the physical organism, and gives use and significance to them all.

The mother takes charge of the germ of a new life. No organized structure is there; only a simple cell, with a something in it, capable, under the action of a power within itself and in the mother, of being developed into a perfect human being. Within nine months that germ appears a living, human body and soul; the growth of the latter having kept exact pace with that of the former. When the eye and ear are perfected, the soul sees and hears; when the brain and nerves are perfected, the soul thinks and feels; when the legs and tongue are perfected, the soul walks and talks; the growth of the psychical corresponding with that of the physical, and the manifestations of the former are essentially controlled by the conditions of the latter. The psychical organism, in all its parts and powers, must, like the physical, be made complete before birth, or it never can be perfected in this state. If the child is born without a physical eye, ear, tongue, arm or leg, these can never be added afterwards. So if any organ, faculty, or power of the psychical organism be incomplete at birth, it must remain so till the dissolution of the body. Whether the inherited, organic diseases and deformities of the psychical organism can be and will be cured after that event, is a fearful question to those who are to be the mothers and fathers of this world's future, if the positions laid down in this work be true. Human souls are cursed, before birth, with painful diseases and horrible deformities. Who does it? The parents; mainly the mother, aided by the father, acting through her. Will those diseases of the soul ever be cured, if not before, then after the dissolution of the body? Mothers! Fathers! Must your outraged, diseased, suffering children stand forever before you, as swift witnesses against your wilful ignorance, your cruel indifference, your ungoverned passion and your inhuman selfishness? Will you not all combine your efforts to purify the fountain from which must issue all the streams of human life that are to flow on and on forever? Will you not, calmly and earnestly, consider the relation of woman's organism to the destiny of the race, and then do whatever may and can be done, to purify and perfect this source, from which have come in the past, and must come in the future, all the psychical, as well as physical human organisms, all the souls as well as bodies, that are to fill and crowd this portion of God's great kingdom, both in and out of the body?

For there is the same reason to conclude that the elements of which souls are made, come from the blood of woman, as well as those of which bodies are made. We have no apparatus to analyze the psychical, as we have to analyze the physical organism. We cannot subject the elements of which souls are made to the scrutiny of the bodily senses. Yet, as both organisms are developed by the action of the plastic or forming power in the maternal organism, and amid the same surroundings, there is the same reason to conclude that both are derived from the same source; that, as the physical eye and ear are derived from the maternal blood, so the psychical power to see and hear, comes from the same; and as the physical brain, nerves and heart, are derived from woman's blood, the psychical power to think and feel, to reason and to love, to will and to do, come from the same source.

Through the action of the mother's blood, life and sensation are communicated to every part, not only of her own system, but also to that of her forming child. As, through

the action of her blood her own organism is prepared to
see, hear, taste, smell, think and feel, and to live and move ;
so through the action of the same agent, her child's organization is perfected, and rendered capable of seeing, hearing,
thinking, feeling, living and acting.   Not only are the physical instruments of thought and feeling, of seeing and hearing, prepared by the action of her blood, but the organization
of the agent, or soul, that is to use those instrumentalities, is
perfected by the same process.

The conclusion is, that there are the same reasons for
believing that there must exist in woman's blood, elements of
which souls as well as bodies are made ; and that there is
power in the germ to gather up and put together those
materials into living human organisms, capable of all the
phenomenal manifestations usually seen and expected in a
human being.   The conclusion seems rational and philo-
sophical, that human beings, with all their essential and
peculiar attributes and characteristics, derive their organic
existence directly from the blood of woman.   Our physical,
intellectual, affectional, and passional predeterminations, come
to us, mainly, through the maternal organism ; and, as are its
conditions, so will be our organization, and, consequently,
our post-natal destiny.

The question may arise, Has woman the power to say of
what materials her blood shall be composed?   Who can doubt
it?   It is to ask, Has woman any power over the quality and
quantity of her food?   That her blood is formed from whatever she takes into her system as nourishment, or as a gratification of her appetite ; that it is characterized, and made
pure or impure, by the quality of what she takes ; that it
may be rendered more or less diseased by the quantity, as
well as by the quality of her food ; that her blood may be
made impure, and rendered unfit to supply healthful nutrition

to her embryo child, by an excess in quantity of even the most healthful food; that she has power to select from the articles spread by God, so bountifully on his great table, selecting that which, in her view, is best adapted to form pure, and rejecting that which is most likely to form impure blood; that the quality of the air she breathes, and the water and liquids she drinks, and the kind and amount of the labor she performs, will materially affect the conditions of her blood; that she can, to a great extent, control the air she breathes, the liquid she drinks, and the labor she performs; that these, and many other things pertaining to her physical life, that essentially affect the character of her blood, are, to a greater or less extent, under her control, none can doubt. If, then, she has power over her food, and over whatever constitutes her nutrition, she has power to say of what her blood shall be made.

Who shall instruct woman in two things? (1.) What materials are best adapted to form the most healthful, vigorous and perfect organization for her child? (2.) What kinds of nourishment are best adapted to supply her blood with those materials? The true woman would become a mother. She would give to her child a healthful, vigorous and happy organism, body and soul. She knows its organic existence must be derived from her blood. Her natural and most anxious inquiry will be, "How can I place my blood in the best possible condition to furnish my child with materials for the best possible organization? Who will instruct me how to make the fountain pure and perfect, from which the organic existence, the character and destiny of my child are to flow?" Who, by chemical analysis, will tell that anxious woman what nutriment is adapted to furnish the best materials for the formation of the most healthful body? Can any

4*

one inform her what nutriment contains most of those elements that are required to form the most perfect soul?

But these are questions for the future of the race in that
good time coming; when, in religion, in morals, in anthropology, and in all efforts to elevate and perfect the nature we
bear, Fiction shall give place to Fact.   In that future, I am
certain the question will be asked and answered — How can
the most healthful, beautiful and happy organic existence be
secured to each child as a birthright inheritance?   Then the
church, the state, the pulpit, the press and platform, and all
who would elevate and save the race, and secure to all a
noble character and a happy destiny, will turn their attention
to the HEALTH OF WOMAN.   All will say — " Let us purify
and perfect her blood, the fountain of all organic life and of
character and destiny to man; let us invigorate, beautify,
ennoble and perfect that organism in which all of human kind
receive their organic existence and direction, their tendencies
to physical disease or health and mental and moral aptitudes ;
let us cleanse and purify the fountain of organic life, and then
the streams that flow from it will be pure."

But, what of the present condition of that fountain of life,
character and destiny to man?   Who can think of it without
shrinking with horror from the ghastly diseases and crimes
that are to flow from it, and the wretchedness that must follow in their train?   Where is the healthy woman?   Where
the mother that rejoices in the perfectly healthful organism of
her child?   *The Blood of Woman!*   It is filled with many
foul diseases.   Of necessity, must not those human organisms
that derive their existence from such a source, be filled with
disease from the crown of the head to the sole of the foot?
What use in trying to heal these wounds and diseases, while
the fountain is left untouched?   The fountain is full of
animal and vegetable putrefaction, all dark and turbid with

filth and corruption. Would we purify the stream? Go then and remove the decaying animal and vegetable substances from the fountain; cleanse it of all that corrupts and pollutes its waters, and makes them poisonous and loathsome; and then clear and beautiful streams will issue from it to gladden and bless all who approach and partake of them. So let the world deal with the Blood of Woman, — purify, beautify and ennoble that, and then nought but cleanliness, purity, beauty and nobleness can flow from it.

CHAPTER IX.

INHERITED MATERNAL CONDITIONS.

Two facts have been stated and commented on, going to show the power of the mother over the organization of the child, i. e. : (1.) The organic existence of the child is begun and completed within the organism of the mother. (2.) The elements of which that organism is composed must come from the mother's blood. These two facts cannot be disputed. A third fact is no less certain, i. e. :

Fact Third. — THE MATERIALS OF WHICH THE CHILD IS COMPOSED, MUST COME FROM THE MATERNAL BLOOD, STAMPED WITH ITS CONDITIONS.

The conditions of woman may be considered in two aspects. (1.) *Physical* conditions.   (2.) *Psychical* conditions, — or conditions of the *body* and conditions of the *soul*. That the conditions of her entire physical organism are in accordance with and indicated by the conditions of her blood, will not be doubted. As is the state of her blood, so will be that of her brain, her heart, her lungs, stomach, liver, and nervous system ; of her eyes, ears, skin, and of every organ and function of her body. Inasmuch as the entire physical structure is nourished and sustained through the blood, and every waste in the tissues and fibres is supplied from the same source ; and that which supplies her own system with nourishment, must supply the materials to form the organism of her embryo child; consequently the impurities and diseases that are in her blood must enter, not only into her own, but also into its body. Her blood must furnish all the materials necessary to form the brain, the lungs, the heart, eyes and ears of her child; and if those materials are defective and diseased, before they are extracted from her blood, they must be so after they are constructed into these different organs, and of course the organs themselves will be defective, and unfitted healthfully to perform the parts assigned to them in the system.

An Authenticated Fact. The following well-attested fact is, in several respects, very illustrative, especially of the power of the maternal blood over the physical conditions of the child, before and after birth. A Mrs. —— gave birth to twins. The physical organisms of the children were perfect and healthful in every part. Such were the conditions. of the mother that it was thought advisable to feed rather than nurse them at the breast. Cows' milk was the only nourishment given them. Though plump, and apparently healthy, their food afforded no nourishment. They would eat voraciously, but they seemed to have no power to convert their food into blood, and thence into bone, brain, and various organs of the body. From the first they began to grow poor, thin, craving and devouring the food, but deriving no means of growth and strength from it. They became very emaciated. At length the attending physician, though he could discover no disease in them, gave them up, declaring that they must die. A neighbor called in to see them, who had given much thought to the subject of animal chemistry and the phenomena of physical life. He saw that the children were starving to death, and that they had no power to convert their food into blood, and appropriate it to the purpose of nutrition. On questioning the mother as to her habits of

life in regard to diet, he found that she had, from early
girlhood, lived mainly on animal food. He inferred that the
trouble was in the food, and not in the children. He said
"the mother's blood was made of *animal* food, and, consequently, the organisms of the children were composed of
materials derived from animal food; and cows' milk, being
the product of *vegetable* food, was not suitable nourishment
for children whose physical existence is derived from animal
food." Accordingly he sent to the market, got a piece of
fresh, tender, lean beef, had some beef-tea made, and, in a
weak state at first, gave some to the famished little ones.
The very smell of it seemed to invigorate them. They lived
on it for weeks, having it made stronger and stronger, till
they were allowed to suck the fibre, and finally to swallow
it. They at once began to grow and strengthen, and in a
few months were hale and hearty. The physical conditions
of the mother were organized into her children, and they
needed food adapted to those conditions. Had they nursed
at the maternal breast, all had been well; but, being fed on
a substance derived solely from vegetable food, there was not
power in them to convert it into nutrition for their peculiar
organisms.

Another Attested Fact, going to show the same. A Mrs.
—————— gave birth to a child, which she could not nurse, and
had to feed. The mother had taken meat and potatoes, and
other hearty vegetables, as a constant diet for years. She
fed her child on tapioca and rice, prepared with cows' milk.
It grew but little in size and weight, and seemed sickly,
weak, and unable to sustain life. After several months, the
mother was persuaded to change its diet, and feed it on
meat, potato, and other hearty vegetables. The child, at
once, began to show the effects of the change, and to become
strong and vigorous. Its nutrition was similar to that on

which its development depended before birth. It is a wise arrangement, doubtless, and founded in true philosophy, that the infant, sometime after it is born, is to derive its nourishment from the maternal organism; thus, in its tenderest and most susceptible period of post-natal existence, deriving its means of growth from the same source from which it derived its nutrition for pre-natal development. Of what is the maternal blood composed? Learn this, and you know what the child, whose organic existence is derived from it, needs to supply its demands. After its birth, the child's body will need to be nourished by substances similar to those on which it was nourished before its birth.

If scrofula, cancer, consumption, or any disease exists in the maternal blood, those diseases, or tendencies to them, must, of necessity, be organized into the body of her child. Within my knowledge, the mother of four children died of consumption. Three of her children, daughters, died of the same disease, at about the age of twenty. The fourth, a son, yet lives, but shows, unmistakably, that he is soon to pass within the veil, by the same disease. Who killed these children? It is a mere convenient fiction, to screen parents from responsibility, to charge their disease and corporeal death, upon God. As well make God responsible for the atrocities of slaveholders, who separate husbands and wives, parents and children, brothers and sisters, who whip and scar the backs of women, and who, as inhuman slave-traders, chattelize and sell men, women and children. The God of Nature is no more responsible for the inherited diseases of those children, than for the blow of the midnight assassin, or the slaughter of men on Bunker Hill, and at Sebastopol. Consumption lurked in the maternal blood, and it was organized into those children before they were born.

The following fact is within my knowledge. A mother of a large family, whose organism was derived from maternal ancestors in whose blood consumption lay concealed, and which culminated in death, had her hopes blasted, and her life deeply saddened, by the death of five of her children by the fell destroyer. She had about the healthiest, most energetic, and all-enduring womanly organism I ever heard of. She lived over three score years and ten, and died without any particular disease or pain. Tendency to consumption may have been in her blood, but no outward symptoms of it ever appeared. How came her children to have it? They may have inherited a tendency to it from her, but the true cause was, the mother was overworked during their prenatal life, and the vital forces and energies that should have been free to give vigor to their organizations, were directed into other channels. The conditions of her blood were poor and feeble, and this feebleness and impotency were organized into them, and they were victimized to her misdirected energies. Her blood, exhausted by her incessant, wearing toil, became inactive, and wholly unfit to impart vitality and energy to her children. During that period, so replete with destiny to the child, the maternal energies should be left entirely free to impart vitality, power and activity, to its organism.

The physical life and condition of every child, and of every man and woman, is proof that the materials which go to form the pre-natal organic existence of children, must be stamped with the conditions of that maternal blood from which they are derived. WOMAN! think of this as you weaken, taint, and pollute your blood with foul narcotics, with nauseous condiments and compounds, with putrid air, with diseased food, with exhausting labors, and with wearying and unnatural, though exciting amusements and indulgences. Hearken!

the anguish and agonies, the wails and woes, of frightful diseases and premature deaths to unborn millions fill the air around you. If you would open your eyes, and unstop your ears, you might see and hear them. Women of the Present and to be the Mothers of the Future! listen to the agonizing prayers that come up to you from the generations whose organisms are to be derived from your blood, and for their sake, purify and keep pure this fountain of life to coming ages. Let no indiscreet, extravagant and unnatural action of yours pollute or enfeeble your blood, and through that mar the beauty or harm the destiny of their physical natures.

But what of the Psychical Conditions of the Mother? That her bodily conditions are organized into her child, is a fact, known and read of all, as a general law of reproduction. How is it with her mental, social· and moral, or psychical conditions? Do these become the inheritance of the child by a similar law? Is her soul as well as her body, the immortal as well as the mortal, the spirit as well as the flesh, the thoughts and feelings as well as the cancers and scrofulas, the psychical as well as the physical diseases and tendencies of the mother, organized into her children? This question is more complicated and comprehensive than the other, and far less easy of a satisfactory solution ; yet, facts in regard to it, are as abundant and intelligible ; and, if we allow ourselves to be guided by these facts, and trace results to antecedents in this as in the physical phenomena of life, our conclusions will be the same.

The conditions of the blood are, to a great extent, controlled by the action of the soul. Certain actions of the mind produce corresponding actions of the blood. The temperature and motions of the blood are heightened and accelerated by the operations of the soul. The character of the thoughts and feelings characterize the action of the blood.

Woman's heart cannot healthfully perform its office, in developing a life-germ into a human being, except as it is filled and thrilled with love for the father of her child. God has imposed on woman this injunction: never to become a mother except under the auspices of a heart entirely permeated and controlled by a concentrated, exclusive, conjugal love for the father of her child. Only such a love, absorbing, filling and thrilling her entire being, can place her blood in a condition adapted to prepare and furnish healthful materials, rightly and happily to construct an organism, truly and nobly to act its part on the theatre of eternity. The action and movements of her blood must obey the pulsations of her heart; the pulsations of her heart must obey the action and emotions of her soul. If her whole soul be vitalized, thrilled, and ennobled by a concentrated, exclusive, conjugal love, that seeketh not its own, and is all-trusting, all-hoping, all-enduring, and filled with all the fulness of God, that will impart health and perfection to the action of her heart, and this will purify, vitalize and quicken the action of her blood; that it may furnish healthful materials to build up the organic structure of her child. Can woman's heart, throbbing with any other emotion, impart such conditions to her blood as are necessary to the formation of a healthful, happy child? But what must be the conditions of that woman's blood, whose heart is cold and dead towards the father of her child, or is excited by bitter antagonism, or anger, or aversion, and with utter disgust towards the relation in which her child originated, or murderous opposition to its existence. God pity the poor child whose organic existence is begun and completed under the action of a heart thus controlled!

CHAPTER X.

THE MOTHER AS A LAWGIVER.

Is it true that human destiny daily and hourly depends on organic conditions and constitutional tendencies?

And is it true that our organic and constitutional tendencies of body and soul depend on maternal conditions?

Behold, then, the empire of woman as a mother! Who shall attempt to estimate its power, its extent and duration? Who shall attempt to calculate its bearing on the destiny of the race, in the body and out of it? What are earthly kings and potentates! They wear a bawble called a crown, and wield a bawble called a sceptre! They rule over states and kingdoms of limited dimensions for a day or an hour. They surround themselves with such splendor as money can buy, and dazzle and bewilder their admirers, and exercise a brief, little authority over them. But who heeds them? Who cares for them? They die corporeally, and are forgotten, and literally, the places and people that once knew them, know them no more, as rulers. How soon their power is taken from them!

How terrible the end of one of the most gorgeous kingdoms earth ever saw!

"And Babylon, the glory of kingdoms, the beauty of the Chaldees' excellency, shall be as when God overthrew Sodom and Gomorrah. It shall never be inhabited, neither shall it be dwelt in from generation to generation. Not even the wild Arab shall pitch his tent there ; nor shall shepherds make their fold there. But wild beasts of the desert shall couch down there ; and their palaces shall be full of doleful creatures. Owls shall hoot there and satyrs dance there. And the wild beasts of the islands shall howl in their desolate houses, and dragons scream in their pleasant dwellings. Lizards and snakes shall crawl over her ruined temples ! Desolation and death shall hold their festival amid her ruins." (Isa. xiii. 19–22.) To the kingdoms of the dead past, this is literally applicable. Neither the model government nor the model man is to be found in the sepulchres of the past. It may in truth be said of all governments of the past, based on military power, with all their array of kings and rulers, — so pass the power and glory of earthly kingdoms and earthly potentates.

But the mother's empire is like that of God's, while absolute in power, it is eternal in duration ! While the human soul exists, it must bear in its nature the imprint and lineaments of the mother.

CONTEMPLATE THE POWER OF THE MOTHER AS A LAW-GIVER ! We are under fixed laws of life and health to body and soul. This is knowledge ; no room is left here for the action of faith. In this we walk by sight, and not by faith. Every plant, every tree, every animal beneath man, is under fixed and just laws of life and health. All that has animal or vegetable life, are brought into existence and carried onward and upward, according to fixed laws. To all eternity we shall be subject to them. Our destiny is fixed, so far as immutable laws can fix it.

Where are these laws to be found? Where is the original, infallible copy? Not in constitutions, codes and creeds, the work of men's hands, but in the body and soul of each man and woman. Each human being, at birth, brings with him or her, as a birthright inheritance, a code of laws, which, if he obeys, he will be all he is capable of being, and just what he was designed to be, and no power in the universe can make him evil or unhappy. But if he disobeys them, no power can make him good and happy while his disobedience continues. No salvation can come to us if we disobey these laws; no condemnation can come to us if we obey them. Health and heaven must result from obedience; disease and hell from disobedience. The penalty is as fixed and certain as the law.

These laws are organized into body and soul, as conditions of life and health. These are the only laws that are ever given to man, by his great Lawgiver. Each is, and ever must be, a law unto himself. No man can be a fixed law unto another. No man can ever make his own will a rule for another. The eyes, ears, tongue, brains, lungs, heart, stomach and blood of one man, can never be governed by any external will or power. The functions of each human organism must be governed by a power within itself. That another eats and drinks, can never assuage my hunger and thirst. That another is truthful, just, and good, can never supply the lack of these qualities in me.

Who is the lawgiver? Who organizes this code of wise and just laws into our existence? Who legislates for us? THE MOTHER, in whose organism our organic existence is begun and completed, and whose tender love, and anxious, sleepless solicitude, preside over our pre-natal development. She legislates not only for individuals, for a town, a state, nation or kingdom, but also for the race. Her legislation is uniform, and every human being must be subject to it. Will the mother's power ever be appreciated by men and women?

Yes; when Fiction shall yield to Fact, and Anthropology become the only Theology.

The laws enacted by her are engraven, not on parchment, nor on wood, nor stone, nor on plates of copper, silver or gold, but on the more enduring substance of the human soul, and also in the body through which that soul is to manifest itself. The mother, as a legislator, organizes the laws of life and salvation into our very existence, makes them essential parts of ourselves; the fixed, unchanging elements of our being. She inscribes them on every nerve, fibre, sinew, tissue, vein, artery, and bone of the body, literally writing them on the heart, stomach, lungs, brain, and every member of the physical organism. Also, on the will, reason, conscience, and every power or faculty of the psychical organism, or soul. She legislates for the interior as well as for the exterior life. The thoughts and affections, and all the unseen, unexpressed operations of the soul, as well as those that are expressed and visible, are awakened and controlled by laws of her enacting. Every element and faculty of our bodies and souls, is absolutely and forever under laws of her enacting; and to each law is annexed the eternal, inexorable fiat — " OBEY AND LIVE ; DISOBEY AND DIE."

These laws of the mother *can never be altered, modified, or repealed.* They are, in truth, the laws of God, and changeless and enduring in all their operations and effects, as the source from which they come. Laws, enacted by states and kingdoms, must be changed or repealed; but the laws enacted by the mother are made essential elements of our existence, and can never be repealed till the entire, human organism, body and soul, is annihilated.

The governments of this world are arbitrary and capricious. They cannot be otherwise. They are one thing to-day, another to-morrow; unstable as the wind or the tide; nothing is fixed or permanent about them. Indeed, the basis of all laws, as enacted by legislators, states and kingdoms, is what ignorant, short-sighted man determines to be present expediency. According to their decisions, what is truth to-day, may be enacted into a lie to-morrow; what is theft, robbery and murder, to-day, may be converted into righteousness to-morrow. The licentiousness of to-day, may become the perfection of moral purity to-morrow. What is truth, justice, mercy, benevolence, kindness, to-day, may be converted into falsehood, injustice, cruelty, and unkindness, to-morrow. Thus are all the enactments of human governments capricious and changeable. They claim the power to annihilate all distinction between good and evil. But the empire of the mother is fixed as the throne of God. Her enactments are for all time and eternity. What is law at one time or place, is law in all times and places. In the code which she gives to her child, as a birthright legacy, what is just in one time and place, is just in all times and places. Her decrees are fixed and unchangeable. Her legislation is for eternity. What is just and right in the body, will be just and right out of it. The laws of the soul, organized into it by the mother, will never be repealed till the soul is annihilated.

There is no partiality in her enactments. Her laws bear on all alike. They ignore all distinction of rich and poor, learned and unlearned, reputable and disreputable, high and low; and they act on all impartially. Before her laws, all are on a dead level. As a subject of law and penalty, she recognizes the absolute equality of man, without regard to color, country, or condition. The laws of civil government are partial. They often act on different persons differently, according as they are rich or poor, high or low, reputable or disreputable. Their penalties are often visited upon criminals according to their color, their wealth, their station, their social standing. But the laws enacted and engraven upon our bodies and souls by the mother are just and impartial, and their penalties visited on all alike, ignoring all adventitious distinctions. Her legislation is for humanity; and all that are human by virtue of their existence as human beings, must be subject to and alike affected by it. " Obey and live — disobey and die," is the only alternative for all. I repeat, *all are equal*, before her enactments. She, as a lawgiver, knows no distinction between rich and poor, enslaved and enslaver, black and white, titled and untitled, popular and unpopular.

The Empire of the Mother is Internal, that of Civil Governments is External. The kingdom of the mother is within us — all other kingdoms are without. The affections, the thoughts, the likes and dislikes, the desires, the passions, the dispositions, the proclivities, the entire health and life of the soul is under the jurisdiction of the mother, as well as the health and life of the body. Civil governments can take cognizance only of the outward, overt acts of the body. The interior life of every human being is subject to her dominion. Victoria's empire as a mother will grow and increase in extent and duration, when her empire as a queen will be forgotten.

Is it said, the mother is not the real lawgiver, but only the agent or medium through which the laws are given? Granted — but has not the mother power to alter or modify the laws of God, as she inscribes them on the child? She may, with those divine laws, organize into her child, certain antagonistic, temporary regulations, which may greatly impede the results which the divine laws are adapted to work out. So that in her child there may be two opposing forces or sets of laws; two conflicting powers or kingdoms. So that each may say, " I find in my members a law, warring against the law of my mind, leading me into captivity to sin. When I would do good, evil is present."

God legislates for men through the mother, never through congress or parliament; nor through the church or state. The laws, given through the mother, are more fitted to work out our glory, than laws given through priests, politicians, ecclesiastical councils, or political caucuses. Woman, as a mother, is the law-making power of the great human kingdom; and the sole legitimate business of all agents, employed to keep the peace, is to see to it that her laws are obeyed; for her laws are the laws of God. The sovereignty of the race is vested in her. God has put into her hand the sceptre of universal dominion. Over every tribe, state, nation, and kingdom, her laws extend; and all peoples, savage and civilized, barbarian and Christian, are under the jurisdiction of the mother. Wherever there are souls to feel and think, to suffer and enjoy, whether in or out of the body, there her power is felt; and her kingdom is an everlasting kingdom, and her dominion limited only by human life.

Thus the mother organizes into the body and soul of her child fixed laws or conditions of health and life. Sad it is, that, at the same time she should, owing to her ignorance and diseased conditions, organize into her child conditions of disease and death; conditions which impel the child to disobedience to these just and wholesome laws, and to a course of non-compliance with those fixed conditions of health and life. Love, justice, truth, forgiveness, forbearance, gentleness, are made essential elements of existence in the soul of her child; at the same time, she organizes into it a propensity to hatred, injustice, falsehood, revenge, and cruelty. *Good for evil*, is the noblest, most essential condition of happiness to her child's psychical existence; yet, with this most essential and absolute law of life, she organizes into it the base and bloody law of retaliation; an almost ungovernable tendency to *evil for evil*. She is taught that her child is a child of God;

5

created in his likeness, and born in his image ; at the same
time, she is taught that her child, if she has one, must be
" conceived in sin, shapen in iniquity, prone to evil, and sent
away from its birth speaking lies." But, who conceives her
child in sin? Who shaped it in iniquity? Who gave it a
proneness to evil? Who sent it away from the birth speaking
lies? These natural and simple questions, religions and
governments, and ministers in church and state have never
attempted to ask nor answer. But while woman, body and
soul, is so fearfully and fatally diseased, she must and will
organize her diseased as well as her healthful tendencies into
her children. She will organize love and hate, forgiveness and
revenge, justice and injustice, good and evil, health and disease, heaven and hell, into her child. But, *health is the law*,
to body and soul; disease the exception. Justice, love,
truth, good for evil, all that is included in the word of God,
is the permanent; their opposites are the transient, and must
pass away. The God, in man, lives and reigns; let the race
rejoice. Let all " *Hope on, and hope ever.*"

CHAPTER XI.

THE MOTHER AS A TEACHER.

SHE is our teacher, not only after we are born, but before; and the pre-natal lessons of the mother are much more potent in their influence on our destiny, than her post-natal instructions.

" What college had the honor of being your *Alma Mater?* " was once asked me in Scotland. " The organism of my mother," said I, " was my primary school, my academy, my college, my university, and the only college from which I ever graduated. The only diploma I ever had was signed and sealed by my mother, as president of that educational institution. That diploma empowered me to live, to think, to feel, and act my part on the theatre of eternity." ALMA MATER! Dear mother indeed to me! The lessons inscribed on my body and soul by thee can never be erased or forgotten. The teachings of priests and politicians, of church and state, of pulpits and platforms, of books and creeds, may be forgotten; but thy lessons, dear mother! are imperishable as the soul on which they are written.

The character of that college, and the lessons taught there, are of more importance to the race, than are those of all other colleges. As an educational institution or power, the maternal organism is more important to mankind, than all educational institutions that human power can set up. That institution over which the mother presides, and whose instructions are in her keeping, is the one great educational power of the world. Before it, all others are but as dust in the balance ; a drop in the ocean. It controls our hourly, daily and eternal destiny. The lessons of all other teachers may be erroneous, and forgotten ; but her instructions, given in our pre-natal life and education, are unerring, and can never be forgotten.

Would that the mother, as the great teacher of the race, were more perfectly prepared to give lessons of love, of wisdom, and eternal life to all of human kind. *The pre-natal Education of Man !* This will one day be regarded as the most important subject to which Religions and Governments can direct attention. In this work both parents must be the teachers ; more especially the mother ; and no pains will be spared to qualify them to give lessons of Love and Wisdom, and not of Hate and Folly ; lessons that lead to God and Heaven, and not that lead to degradation and misery.

What is done, what can be done, to qualify the mother to be the teacher of truth, and only truth, to the race. It is of moment that she be duly qualified to fill the station of a wise, loving, unerring teacher. Where are the normal schools at which woman may be instructed and qualified, as a mother, to become the lawgiver and teacher of the race? Are there none in which woman may be taught her true relations to the destiny of that race of beings, of which she is the mother? Governments and .churches found schools and colleges to educate men and prepare them to be lawyers, doctors, priests, statesmen, legislators, judges, and rulers ; but, what have they done to found schools and colleges to educate women in *the divine, the august science of Maternity ?* Geology, chemistry, botany, geography, geometry, theology ; these, and other sciences, are sedulously taught by church and state ; but not a school has church or state ever founded to teach woman that science in which is wrapt up the destiny of individuals, of states, nations, and kingdoms, and of the race, i. e., THE SCIENCE OF MATERNITY. Alas! for the folly, the stupidity, the insanity of that state or church that spares no labor or expense, to educate men and women to teach a district school (a most laudable object), or to legislate for, or rule over a petty state or kingdom, but bestows not a thought, nor a dollar to educate her for her divine mission as a mother, who is the teacher and legislator of the race, and whose lessons and legislation take hold on eternity. What labor, what anxiety, what self-denial are practised by fathers to educate their sons to fill a professorship in some petty college! But what is done by those fathers to educate their daughters to be competent professors in that college from which must be graduated or come forth, all the individuals, and the states and kingdoms of this world's future? Nothing! alas! NOTHING!

Woman, as a mother, under God, is the author of that constitution and code of laws by which the destiny of every individual man and woman, and every church, state, nation and kingdom, must be decided. Let her be taught how to engrave that constitution and code on each human body and soul, unmixed with organic diseases, and inherited tendencies, appetites and passions, that must necessarily impede the true and healthful action of those fixed and just laws. Let her be so educated that she may impart to her child, in its prenatal life, the lessons that must lead it up to whatever of beauty, purity, greatness and glory, it shall ever attain, without intermingling with them lessons and tendencies that necessarily lead to deformity, impurity and infamy. Now, while the mother inscribes health on the body, as the law of its being, she also organizes into that body tendencies to various and painful diseases; and while she inscribes on the soul lessons of wisdom, love, justice, truth, forgiveness and self-sacrifice, she also organizes into it tendencies to hatred, injustice, falsehood, revenge and selfishness. Thus, mainly through ignorance, the mother lays the foundation in her child, of a life-long and desperate conflict with itself. Thus, the child, in far distant periods of its existence, is victimized to maternal ignorance, and in agony of spirit, is made to cry out, " when I would do good, evil is present ! "

In the name of humanity, let woman be taught how to furnish herself with the best possible materials, of which to construct the human organism, the most delicate, complicated and wonderful of all structures ; and then let her be taught how to put those materials together, so as to form the most perfect human being. Thus let her be qualified to be to individuals, states and kingdoms, " the way, the truth, and the life."

THE MOTHER A PRIEST.

Yes ; God's true, anointed, and ordained priest, to minister at the great altar of humanity. From the hour in which she takes charge of the germ of a new life, she stands before the present and the future of this world, and in presence of eternity, with its unending years, and its ceaseless progression, arrayed in robes of light, as God's high priest to her child. Truly, in presence of the unconscious immortal that is being developed beneath her loving heart, she stands clothed with light as with a garment. A crown of glory is on her head, a diadem of beauty encircles her brow, and she awaits the hour, the *coronation* hour, when she can place that crown of glory upon the head of her child, and encircle its brow with that diadem of beauty, and start it on a career of eternal life and unending progression under happy auspices.

No oracles of Apollo are so true, and so sure to come to pass. No priest ever stood so near to God, and to the objects of his ministrations as she does. No prayers are ever offered so earnest, so deep, so agonizing, as those offered by the mother, the great high priest of God, in behalf of the dear one that is being developed beneath her loving, anxious heart. The ever earnest call of her soul unto God is, that her babe may be blest and filled with all the fulness of God. That her child may be born with a healthy body and soul, adorned with grace and beauty, and ever grow in favor with God and man. Thus, with tenderest love and heroic fortitude, she prepares herself for the august martyrdom of maternity; and proudly and joyfully lays her life on the altar of sacrifice, with a "GLORIA IN EXCELSIS" in her heart and on her lips.

To her unborn babe she daily and hourly delivers oracles, direct from the heart of God. She stands, as it were, in the place of God, to her unborn babe. Men are educated by the church, to fill the office of priest, and to administer at what is called the altar of God, i. e., to baptize, to administer sacraments, to pray, to preach, and act as go-betweens between God and the people. Ecclesiastical councils license and ordain these priests. All religions have their priests; but the mothers of the race are its true, God-ordained priest-hood. God calls the mother to the office of the priest, to be his minister, his High Priest to enter the very Holy of Holies, where is the ark of the covenant; and there, in his name, to administer to the embryo man or woman, not by reading and expounding what others have said and done, but by organizing into its very being a code of fixed, unchanging laws or conditions of life and health. She stands between God and her unborn babe, to administer to it the image and glory of God.

CHAPTER XII.

THE MOTHER AS A PROPHET.

WHO but the mother is competent to read the future of earth's sons and daughters? She sees their future of weal or woe in her own experiences during their pre-natal life. No need for her to consult the stars, to learn her child's destiny; let her consult her own conditions of body and soul, between the conception and birth of her child. No need to look into some divining glass, nor to consult the flight of birds, nor other mysterious omens and oracles; let her look into the mirror of her own internal experience. In that, as in a divination glass presented to her by God, the Great Divinator, she may see the future of her child, and foretell its destiny, as surely as she can see effects in causes, in any department of life. If certain conditions are present in the mother, corresponding results must follow in the child. Like produces like; health produces health, disease, disease; love produces love, hatred, hatred.

Religion teaches that God, through Moses, David, Isaiah, Paul, and other prophets, made known what was to be in the distant future. But far more surely does he make known through the mother the future character and destiny of individuals and nations. For in maternal conditions hath God written the future of the race.

In the highest sense is the mother the true prophet of God to the race; and the Divine origin of her commission cannot be doubted. In her conditions is written the fate of kingdoms and empires, as well as of individuals. In her experience during the pre-natal life of man, the mother can speak to coming ages, and, in the name of God, pronounce their doom for weal or woe.

The throbbings of her heart are prophetic of the throbbings of her child's heart, in the far distant future. In her own thoughts, plans and purposes, she may see its thoughts, plans and purposes, as it speeds on its pathway of immortality. Her likes and dislikes, her loves and hatreds, her attractions and repulsions, and her sympathies, are but a prophecy, sure and unerring, of what will be the loves and hates, the attractions and repulsions, and sympathies of her child, when its life shall be blended with the life of the Past in the spirit state. In her vanity, her ambition, her selfishness, her irritability, her anger, her revenge, she may see and foretell the doom of her child in regard to such manifestations. In short, in her conditions and manifestations of her intellectual, social, moral, affectional and passional nature, during the pre-natal life of her child, she may read that child's intellectual, social, moral, affectional and passional destiny, as it mingles with its fellow-beings, and with them struggles onward and upward in its career of eternal life. My mother! My mother! What wast thou to me, as my organic existence was being perfected under the pulsations of thy gentle, loving heart, and from materials derived from thy blood, but a prophecy of my character and my destiny, both in and out of the body. Thy son will ever bless and honor thee for the measure of health and happiness, to body and soul, which thou didst mete out to him as his birthright inheritance. During his sixty-five years of experience in life, he has not been called to one week of suffering that deserves the name. What little of diseased and inharmonious action of his physical organism he has

5 *

experienced, has been easily and speedily rectified by the energetic, living, ever-present and ever-watchful Recuperator or Redeemer thou didst organize into him. Thanksgiving to thee, my loving mother! and the voice of melody will ever fill my heart for the life of almost uninterrupted health and happiness thou didst organize into me. Under God, "thine shall be the glory forever," for this great salvation, and for the inestimable gift of an inborn Saviour so vigilant, and so energetic to save.

The throbbings of the mother's heart are prophetic, not only of the destiny of individuals, in their distant future, but also of the character and destiny of states and kingdoms. As are the individuals composing them, so are states and nations. As shall be the individual men and women of the future, so will be the states and nations of the future. The power that determines the character and destiny of the individuals of the future, must also determine the character and destiny of the governments and nations of that future. The power that holds in its keeping, the life and happiness of individuals, holds in its keeping the life and prosperity of nations.

Where-are the men and women of the future? As yet they are not. Whence are they to come? From the organism of woman, that fountain of organic life, from which all the countless millions of human beings that are to people this planet in the coming ages, are to derive their existence, their vitality, and their innate proclivities. From the feminine organisms of the present, are to proceed the men and women who are to establish and administer the governmental and ecclesiastical establishments of the future; who are to give existence and character to all the literary, commercial, social, political and religious institutions that are to do their part in moulding the domestic and social relations of coming generations. And what is the condition of these organisms in which is wrapt up the destiny of this world's future? The organism of woman! That fountain of life, character and destiny to the race! What is its present state? In it are all the elements of a healthy, noble, glorious life and destiny to the individuals and nations of the future; but how mixed up with elements of every foul disease and suffering, and of vice, discord, tyranny, and every crime. Deriving existence from such a diseased fountain, what appalling scenes of human wretchedness must be the doom of the world's future.

See that maternal heart under whose pulsations and aus- pices the organic existence of Napoleon was begun and completed. Every pulsation of that mother's heart, during the pre-natal life of her child, was prophetic of the rise and fall of kingdoms and empires; the watchword of revolution. Europe bowed to the pulsations of that maternal heart, and confessed that her destiny for ages, hung upon its decisions. The thoughts, feelings, hopes and aspirations of that mother's soul gave tone and character to the pulsations of that mater- nal heart. The throbbings of that heart controlled the con- ditions of that maternal organism. The conditions of that maternal organism controlled the physical, intellectual, social and spiritual conditions of the child, and of the future Empe- ror and warrior. That mother, in her own experiences during the pre-natal life of her son, might have read the fate of Europe in the far distant future, had she known how to interpret them.

A FACT. — The following sad incident occurred in my experience. I had lectured in a country town in New England, on the pre-natal life and education of man. A woman, a mother with her son of three years old, called upon me. I was much interested in her boy, so perfect in its physical organization. The child stepped out of the

room, attracted by other children. To the mother, I said,
" What a healthy, noble boy you have. One of whom any
mother might well be proud." To my amazement, she,
bursting into tears, exclaimed, " I long and pray for his
death ! It would be an infinite relief to me to lay that form,
so healthy, strong and perfect, in the grave." " Your conduct," I replied, " seems most unnatural and monstrous."
" I know it must seem so to you, sir, still I long to see him
draw his last breath in childhood, for so surely as he lives,
he will become a murderer, and meet the murderer's doom
on the gallows." " On what do you base your unmotherly,
unnatural prophecy ? " I asked. " On my own conditions
before his birth," said she ; " from his conception to his birth,
I longed and labored for his death. I did all I could and
dared to do, to kill my child without killing myself. My
heart was filled with the spirit of murder against the life of
my child. He struggled into life against the spirit of murder
in the heart of his mother. That he was born a living child
was my deepest anguish, for, too truly, my spirit foreboded
what he must be, whose pre-natal life and education was
completed beneath a heart whose every throb was a threat
of death, and a protest against its existence." " But," I
asked, " does his post-natal life thus far correspond with your
conditions during his pre-natal life ? " " Oh, too truly, too
fatally," said the weeping mother ; " I cannot awaken in him
the least sympathy and consideration for the persons of
others. He is utterly callous about inflicting wounds and
death on others. If his parents, or any body, offend him, he
strikes at their faces or persons, with whatever sharp or
deadly weapon he may happen to have, or that lies within
his reach. I dare not leave him alone with other children,
for fear he will kill them. God forgive me ! " cried the poor
mother, " I knew not what I was doing ! I knew not that

my conditions were being stamped on my poor, unconscious, unborn child!"

See Christendom paying homage to the spirit and life of Jesus! That spirit and life were the natural results of the conditions of that maternal organism in which his organic existence was begun and completed. Had she known how to read results in their antecedents, what a future for the race might not the mother of Jesus have seen in her physical, intellectual, social, and spiritual conditions, during his gestational life! The pulsations of her heart had been to her prophetic of the time when violence should cease, when the nations of the earth should recognize her unborn child as "King of kings, and Lord of lords," and "the kingdoms of this world should become the kingdoms of our God;" and the "Lord God Omnipotent reign" over all the earth, through his vicegerent — THE MOTHER.

CHAPTER XIII.

THE MOTHER AS A MESSIAH.

THE work to be done is, TO ELEVATE AND PERFECT HUMAN NATURE. This can be done only in one way, i. e., by curing the human organism of its diseases, and bringing it into a healthy state in all its functions. HEALTH IS HEAVEN, DISEASE IS HELL. Man will find no hell, except the hell he carries in him. Wherever we go, if we carry hell, we shall find it. How can hell be expelled from the human organism? Expel disease, and the work is done. Bring that organism into a state of healthy, harmonious action, in all its relations, and man is saved from hell and raised to heaven. Heal body and soul of their diseased and discordant action, and the man is saved in the only sense in which he can be. He is rescued from a hell-state, and placed in a heaven-state.

WE FIND WHAT WE CARRY. If we carry cancer, dyspepsia, neuralgia, consumption, or other physical diseases, we shall find *physical* hell wherever we go. If we carry anger, wrath, hate, revenge, jealousy, envy, suspicion, ambition, or other psychical diseases, we shall find a *psychical* hell wherever we go, whether in the body or out of it. And this is the only salvation, i. e., to rescue the human being from a diseased, or hell-state, and bring it into a healthy, or heaven-state.

On whom, above all others, has God imposed this work of rescuing man from disease and suffering, and elevating him to health and heaven? Whom has God appointed to this work of saving the race? Whom has he sent on this mission of redemption, this embassy of love and mercy to the human family? The work to be done is simple and easily comprehended, i. e., to cure the human organism of its diseases. Who is the God-appointed physician to perform this cure, and thus to be the true Messiah and Saviour of the race? All nature answers, — THE MOTHER. No being can hold a relation to the human family so intimate and so potential as she does. The three facts to which attention has been called, cannot be true of any other being ; i. e. : —

1. THE ORGANIC EXISTENCE OF EVERY HUMAN BEING IS BEGUN AND COMPLETED WITHIN THE ORGANISM OF THE MOTHER.

2. FROM HER BLOOD MUST COME THE MATERIALS OF WHICH EVERY HUMAN ORGANISM IS MADE.

3. WHATEVER DISEASE LURKS IN HER BLOOD MUST BE ORGANIZED INTO HER CHILD.

The destiny of the race is in the hands of the being of whom these facts are true, and who is thus intimately related to every child that is born. We know the entire work of organization must be done under the direction of that plastic power that God has placed in her for this purpose. From conception to birth, such is the relation between the mother and child that every pulsation of her heart, every action of her intellect, and of her affections, sympathies, passions and appetites, bear directly on the organic conditions and constitutional tendencies, and, of course, on the post-natal character and destiny of her child. Whose power, for good or evil, can be so great as the mother's? It is not possible, in the nature of things, for man to wield such power. To this, the facts just stated, touching the relations of the mother to her child and her direct power over it, fully attest. It is not possible for any created being to hold relations with the human race so intimate and wield a power so direct and extensive, as that which is held and wielded by the mother.

In the history of man, every age and nation have those who are regarded as sent of God to heal and save. They are called the Messiahs, the Saviours, or Redeemers of mankind. In all countries and religions are men who are regarded as commissioned and sent of God to heal the human organism of its diseases, and restore it to health; to expel hell from it, and introduce heaven into it; and men are educated, set apart, licensed and ordained as priests and teachers, to point the world to those reputed Messiahs and Saviours, to save them from abnormal acts and their results; or, in other words, to restore healthy action to all our powers of body and soul, in all the relations of life, and to make us the true, loving, gentle, noble and happy men and women we were designed to be, and are capable of being. These Messiahs and the religions taught by them, are of use to mankind, and worthy of regard only so far as they seek to expel, and do expel, disease and hell from the human body and soul, and bring into them health and heaven. None of these Redeemers can possibly exert an influence so direct and potent, over the character and destiny of man, as that which is exerted by the mother. Not one of them can possibly enter into a relation to the physical and psychical organization, the intellectual, social, sympathetic and passional nature of man, so intimate, so direct, so endearing, and so enduring, as that which every mother holds to her child.

Though model characters of the past, — as the incarnations of love, justice, truth, self-abnegation and good for evil, and of fidelity to their own convictions, and unfaltering loyalty to their own higher nature ; though their spirit, if imbibed, and their teachings, if followed, might beautify and ennoble, yet nothing which they have said or done can possibly bear so directly on our interior and exterior life, and on our destiny, as the spirit and teachings and conditions of the mother. No man can be a Saviour, to save us from transgression and its consequences, and form and train us to cease to do evil, and learn us to do well ; no man can be commissioned and sent of God, to set up the kingdom of heaven in the human organism, and inaugurate the reign of " peace on earth and good will among men," as the mother can be and is ; because no man can hold a relation to mankind so direct, so absolute and vitalizing as she must, nor hold in his keeping the character and destiny of the race, in the sense that she does. The mother is to her child, in a sense in which no man can be, " the way, the truth, and the life." As a general rule, the same tendencies must be in the child that are in the mother. As a birthright inheritance, the child must put on the mother, and be clothed with her spirit and conditions of body and soul, more entirely than any other being. The mother, body and soul, must be born into the child, and become a part of its nature, and the governing power of its destiny, in the body and out of it, in a sense in which no other recognized Saviour of the dead past, or of the living present, can possibly be.

We know that health and heaven, or salvation, must result from the operation of the fixed laws of life and health, understood and obeyed. Who is chosen and commissioned of God to inscribe these laws on human bodies and souls? Not man, but woman ; not the father, but the mother. The mother is commissioned, not only to enact, but also to expound and enforce them. Millions of men are trained to go forth and point the world to those who have been received as God-anointed and God-inspired teachers and Messiahs of the past, to learn what these laws are, and find motives to obey them. But what has been done by churches, or states and nations, to teach woman how most perfectly to organize into each child the kingdom of heaven as a birthright legacy, and thus to become true saviours? No pains are spared to teach the young daughters of the race those things which may give them a transient popularity and standing in society ; but what is done to fit them for the one grand and holy mission of their existence, i. e., as mothers, to organize into those whose existence and destiny are to be derived from their organisms, love, justice, truth, purity and heaven ; in a word, health of body and soul, and thus to be the true saviours of human beings — to save them from wrong-doing and its sad results, by enthroning a God of love and justice over the soul of each child, as its only redeeming and governing power during its eternal existence?

THE GOSPEL OF GENERATION — THE GOSPEL OF RE-GENERATION. — Which is the Gospel of God to save the human race from disease and suffering, and give to it health and happiness? The Gospel of Generation proposes to to save the world, and establish on earth the reign of Justice, Freedom, and Fraternity, by having the human organism constructed of sound materials, and by having these healthy materials harmoniously put together in the pre-natal state. The Gospel of Regeneration proposes to accomplish the same end by ignoring Generation as a means of salvation, and pointing to Repentance and Reformation as the only hope of the world; the Gospel of Generation proposes to save the world by having all human beings conceived in love and purity, shapen in the likeness of God, prone to good, and sent away from the birth speaking truth ; the Gospel of Regeneration proposes to reach the same result by Repentance, after they have been "conceived in sin, shapen in iniquity, prone to evil, and sent away from the birth speaking lies." The Gospel of Generation would prevent men from becoming criminals ; the Gospel of Regeneration aims to reform or punish them after crime is organized into them. The former seeks to save by preventing the weeds and tares from getting into the field ; the latter aims to save by trying to dig and root them out after their seeds are sown, and they have taken deep root. The one would save from burning, by keeping human beings out of the fire ; the other would accomplish the same end, by snatching them from the flames after they have been cast into the fire, and have been scorched and nearly consumed by the devouring element.

The mother is sent of God to save the world by organizing the kingdom of heaven into the child before it is born ; and then, after it is born, with the assistance of the father, and other teachers and Messiahs, to develop and perfect that kingdom, and make it the only governing power. The mother is not only designed to be a Saviour herself, but, as such, she is set apart by God to see to it that a true and efficient Saviour, all-competent to save from disease of body and soul, is organized into each child, and made an essential element of its existence. Her mission to her unborn child is, to see to it, that, when her child is born, *a Saviour is born with it and in it.* Her great mission is, to publish to all of human kind " glad tidings of great joy," through a healthy and happy organization ; the mission of all other Messiahs has been to publish the same, through Repentance and Reformation ! The mother, as a Saviour, introduces the child into the kingdom of God, at the first and natural birth ; other Saviours labor to do the same thing by a second and supernatural birth. Which is the wisest, most expedient, and attended with the least risk and suffering, to start a human being right at first, and then, by wise and loving teachings, to keep him right; or to start him wrong, by organizing into him tendencies to wrong, and then, after he is cursed with an all but ungovernable propensity to intemperance, to tyranny, to man-stealing, to prostitution, to injustice, theft, robbery, and murder, and after he has run a course of vice and crime till the heart is callous, reason is darkened, and the voice of conscience hushed, to try to get him right? Better to start the child right and keep it right, than to start it wrong, and then labor to get it right. Better to "beat swords into plough-shares and spears into pruning-hooks," and to teach the world to learn war no more, by organizing into the human soul Love, Forgiveness, and Good for Evil; than to seek the same end, by organizing into it Hatred, Revenge, and Evil for Evil, and then by Penitentiaries and Gallows to try and keep men from acting out these innate propensities to violence and blood. Far, far better to save from drunkenness by organizing into the human soul a taste for pure water, and nothing else, as a beverage, than to organize into it the drunkard's appetite, — a longing for alcoholic, narcotic, and exciting drinks, — and then to try to eradicate that appetite, after it has its poor, besotted victim in its deadly grasp. It is wiser, more natural, more kind, and more certain of success, to guide a soul to heaven by starting it in that direction at the outset of its long and endless journey, than to start it in an opposite direction, and then pray, and preach, and labor to stop it in its hell-bound career, and get it to turn about and struggle against fierce and debasing propensities, to reach that heaven-state designed by God to be its birthright inheritance.

Thus, the Gospel of Generation, is the Gospel of Nature

and of Nature's God; and the mother, owing to the peculiar and most intimate relation which she holds to the pre-natal life and organization of every human being, is designed to be, and can be, the natural Saviour of the race. "God is Love, and he that dwelleth in Love, dwelleth in God, and God in him." A more sublime and comprehensive expression was never uttered. No truth, ever spoken in words, is more vital to the redemption of mankind. To the mother belongs the prerogative and the most august of all missions, of conferring on every human being, as a birthright inheritance, such a nature as will enable him from the outset of life, and during all his course of eternal progression, to embody and actualize, in his own person, the truth, that " to dwell in Love is to dwell in God." Such a nature — which will turn and be attracted to Love and to God, as naturally and necessarily as the needle turns to the Pole — has every child a right to demand of its mother; and the mother, who, for any cause, refuses to organize into her child this salvation, this divine nature, and thus to enstamp upon its soul the pure, unsullied image of God, does it a grievous wrong.

It will be asked, How are those to be saved who "are conceived in sin, shapen in iniquity, prone to evil, and who go away from the birth speaking lies?" All such must be born again. To them the Gospel of Regeneration is the only " glad tidings of great joy." Repentance, Reformation, or Regeneration, is the only door by which they can enter the kingdom of heaven; yet it had been better for them, — had saved them from much suffering, from bitter self-reproach, and shame and anguish, — had they entered the kingdom of God through the door of Generation, with a gentle, loving, tender mother to crown them with glory at their birth, and to fit them out with healthy, vigorous and perfect bodies and souls to enable them to meet bravely and triumphantly whatever obstacles may lie in their pathway of eternal life.

CHAPTER XIV.

THE TRIUMPH OF REASON AND CONSCIENCE.

MAN is not made to be governed by instinct, passion, or appetite. These should ever be under the control of reason and conscience. This should ever be the case with parentage, and the relation that leads to it. Neither man nor woman has a right to inflict pain and suffering on others, especially on their children, for their own gratification. Offspring is a demand of Human Nature. But if the physical and psychical conditions of the husband and wife — or of either of them — be such that this demand of their nature cannot be met without inflicting great wrong and suffering on their child, what ought they to do? Sacrifice themselves by foregoing the fulfilment of that demand, or satisfy this demand at the expense of their children? If a wife cannot become a mother without entailing on her child a frightful legacy of pain and anguish, is it right for her to give existence to a child? Should not the maternal instinct in this case be controlled by reason and conscience? If so, what is their decision?

I would commend the following letter to the attentive perusal of every conscientious man and woman who would bring their entire nature under the government of that God who pleads for justice and right in their own souls, and to whom they pray — " Thy kingdom come ; Thy will be done on earth as it is in heaven." The letter deserves earnest consideration. It is impossible not to respect the earnest and conscientious writer.

"HENRY C. WRIGHT: My Friend, — I have lately been reading your works, entitled 'Marriage and Parentage,' and 'The Unwelcome Child ; ' and the tone of those works has led me to write-you an account of my own experiences; more particularly, as the stand which I have taken has been in a great measure caused by the principles therein advanced. I ask not pardon for the liberty ; you will not require it. The experience of any woman, so far as her maternal instincts are concerned, must be of interest to you ; inasmuch as it is upon known facts that all correct and valuable conclusions must rest ; and any fact must be of service to you. In relating my experience, I shall not feel called upon to fetter myself by any conventional proprieties as they are termed, and in stepping into the broad field which lies beyond mere conventionalisms, I feel that I shall have the approval of every honest and candid spirit, that views these things from their only true stand-point — *their bearing upon the weal or woe of millions yet unborn.*

" I am a wife in the truest sense of the word. God himself has signified to me that such is the case. I have what makes me truly a wife in the sight of God — a consciousness that I love as a wife. This consciousness, 'signed, sealed and delivered' by God himself, is the unmistakable evidence that I am a wife. I love my husband, and that love constitutes me a wife. This consciousness of loving is a renewing of my whole nature. Were it not so, it would not be true conjugal love. True, conjugal love, never yet failed to bring a soul into the kingdom of God. It must bless its subject and its object. It cannot injure the peace of that soul which is

regenerated by it.   Thus a great want in my womanly nature
is met.   The deep, ever-present love of a wife lifts my soul
to God and His Kingdom.   It asks for its reward only its
existence in my soul.   There it rests to bless and to ennoble,
wholly independent of any one outside of myself.   Thus my
womanly nature, in at least one of its elements, is born again,
and saved from ‚the desolation which must ever exist in the
heart of that woman who is unregenerated by the love of a
wife.

" But there is another element stern and mighty in the
nature of every true woman ; more particularly of one born
into the kingdom of conjugal love, i. e., THE DESIRE TO BE
A MOTHER.   The love.of a wife constitutes a wife, but the
desire to be a mother does not constitute a mother ; and as
we never can know of the love of a wife, until it is called into
existence by a husband, so we can never know the height,
depth and breadth, of the love of a mother, until it is called
into conscious existence by a child.   As the failure to reciprocate the love of a wife on the part of the husband does not
affect her love as a wife, so the failure of a child who might
be so unnatural as to fail to reciprocate its mother's love, does
not effect a change in that love.   But once let that love as a
mother be called into existence by a child, and that love will
always remain in the soul of that mother, to lead her onward
and upward.   As I have felt the sacred influences of the
love of a wife, and through it, been made to see ; so do I now
most earnestly call for the consciousness of a mother's love.

" But why cannot I be a mother?   You ask, ' Does not thy
husband respond to this call of thy nature?'   Yes ; he
desires to be the father of my child.   He would meet this
great want of my being and crown me with this great blessing.
But still the precious boon is denied me.   Why?   Because I
CANNOT, I DARE NOT, CURSE MY CHILD WITH MY PHYSICAL

DISEASES. Because justice forbids me to call into being a sickly, diseased child. And yet I am healthier than most women. People look upon me and say, ' What a strong, healthy body you have.' But underneath my present outward health lurks the scourge — *scrofula.* My childhood was, for the most part of it, spent in a body covered with scrofulous sores, affecting my eyesight, causing me to be laid upon the bed of suffering for months, and spending hours which ought to have been spent in God's sunlight, within the walls of a darkened room ; and though, with the help of a strong constitution, its ravages have been partially checked, still, now, it frequently gives tokens of its presence by painful abscesses, which take me down in all my seeming health and strength. Can I give this to my child? Would not the suffering of my child be an ever-present condemnation to me? Think of a helpless child, at first dependent on the blood of its mother for sustenance, and obtaining its life therefrom, during its pre-natal development. Think of the helpless germ of a human being, with no power to choose its place of development, deposited where it can draw nothing but disease and destruction to its physical nature. Think of the child after it is born, trustingly drawing its sustenance from the breast of its mother, and at every breath, drawing sickness and death therefrom. Though I long to press my child to my bosom, to feel that its life depends on the nourishment it receives there, can I do so knowing that that nourishment is full of scrofula and will curse my child !

" My friend ! Pity me you must, for surely I need pity. It is not my fault that I am called upon to take up this cross. My parents, (God forgive them,) without regard for my welfare, brought me into being. Both of them uniting to fill my body with disease. The germ was diseased, and placed in a diseased organism, there to be developed into a body, which

6

became the habitation of a human soul. And this diseased habitation was my birthright inheritance. Hard it would be, even if my parents gave me an existence because they wanted me. But they did not. I was the youngest of a large family of children, not two years between any two of them, and *I was not wanted*, but taken as an unavoidable result, and loved, I doubt not, but I did not have such a welcome into existence as is the birthright of every child.

" With these wrongs I have struggled all my lifetime. How many traits of character, how much peevishness and fretfulness have been fostered in me, which physical suffering alone placed there! But the great struggle, the great battle of life, has come upon me now. Physical suffering I can bear. I had rather bear it than to see my child enduring it. But this desire to be a mother! Never has any thing taken such a complete possession of my whole soul. It is ever present in all my daily life. A child, soul of my soul, life of my life, given to me to develop! The temptation is sometimes stronger than I can resist by my natural powers of conscience. A stronger heart than mine points out the way, and says, ' He that taketh not his cross is not worthy of me.' I should indeed be unworthy the name of wife and mother, if I persisted in meeting this deep want of my being by giving birth to a scrofulous and diseased child. This is the greatest wrong of all which my parents did to me; giving me such an organism as to make this great struggle between affection and duty an ever-present element of my whole life. I never shall be able to quench the desire ; and I should fail to be a woman if I did. Thus the future looms up before me ; a wife but not a mother; an intense longing for a child to speak in loving tones, the word ' Mother ; ' but, alas! no such word, from such lips, can ever greet my ear, unless I wilfully trample upon my sense of justice and right.

"But, thank God! I can endure this trial. I can be true to the voice of God in my own soul, but I cannot, I will not trample upon the heaven-born rights of my child. No such terrible alternative which presents itself to me, shall ever be presented to a child of mine. No suffering, feeble infant of mine shall wail out the wrong I have done it, with its cries of pain and suffering; but, instead, a voice which spoke ages ago, and which is still ready to speak in every human soul that is true to its warnings, speaks to me the same precious words which greeted one of old, ' This is my beloved child, in whom I am well pleased.' And as I mount the cross which my parents in their ignorance reared for me, God grant that this prayer to heaven may come out from the depths of my soul, ' Father, forgive them, for they knew not what they did.'

"And now, my friend! I appeal to you. Which is the way for me? There are three open before me. One is to be the mother of a diseased child. Another is to live with my husband, in all the horrors of a licensed prostitution, — thus desecrating the highest and holiest function of conjugal love to the lowest of purposes. The other is to be true to my sense of justice, and keep my desire to be a mother, in entire subjection to conscience and reason, and never yield to it, until I can honestly do so with the assured hope that the organic existence of my child can be begun and completed amid holy influences and healthy surroundings; blessed with a deep love-nature, and a perfectly healthy body, in which its soul can develop for its eternal existence. Under no other conditions can I become a mother; and as the wrong done to me, by my parents, positively forbids all hope of such conditions, I can never enter into that relation. Priests profess to have power to give me a license so to do; but a voice stronger than thousands of priests thunders its warnings into my soul, if I do.

"Can it be right for a woman wilfully and knowingly to

transmit to a child, diseases which have been the bane of her life? Can it be right for a man to insist upon a woman's so doing?

"Is it right for a woman whose blood is filled with disease to live with a man as her husband, knowing that she is to be compelled to give birth to sickly and suffering children?

"Which course will result in the most happiness, the one that fights against, and refuses to gratify the deep, parental instincts of her nature, and deems the law of conscience stronger than the law of maternity; or the one that lays her sense of justice and right upon the altar of desire, however pure and holy it may be?

"Let the experience which I have written you tell how I have answered these questions. Am I right or wrong?

"The blood of woman! What a fearful state it is in? What can cleanse and purify it, and render it fit to develop and perfect the human organism? What salvation is there for that woman, who, fighting the terrible battle between duty and desire, yields to the latter, and brings forth a living monument to her sin and wrong! Or what salvation is there for her who, being true to conscience, fails to obey that command of God to every woman — 'be a mother,' and in the loneliness and agony of her afflicted heart, she cries out, 'My God, my God, why hast thou forsaken me!' A wife, but not a mother! A mother, but such only of a sickly and diseased child! Such must be the condition of the masses of our women. What power shall lead them to a thorough regeneration, and make them what God designed they should be — *healthy mothers of healthy children!* Can you tell the way? Can you point out the balm and the physician that can purify and cleanse the blood of woman, and by that means save the world from the hell of disease, to body and soul, into which it is sinking?"